OV

Tracker's car was ro
big ten-ton truck mu
Black smoke puffed from the stack. Gears jammed and
crashed in the powerful diesel engine. Spearblades of
light flared from the flatbed at the back.

Under the fusilade of gunfire, the car fishtailed, metal
scraping rock. The windshield disintegrated, cubes of
glass peppering Tracker like birdshot. He tried to shoot
out the driver's cab of the big truck, but it was no good.
The car was weaving too much.

Tracker grabbed the door handle and, holding the machine gun in one hand, jackknifed the door open—and
dove out of the speeding car . . .

SPECIAL PREVIEW!

Turn to the back of this book for a sneak peek at the all-new action series . . .

THE LAST RANGERS

An electrifying novel of high-tech lawmen in the Texas of tomorrow—available from Berkley Books.

The TRACKER series by Ron Stillman

TRACKER

DYNASTY OF EVIL

RON STILLMAN

DIAMOND BOOKS, NEW YORK

This book is a Diamond original edition, and has never been previously published.

DYNASTY OF EVIL

A Diamond Book / published by arrangement with the author

PRINTING HISTORY
Diamond edition / October 1992

ISBN: 1-55773-771-1

Diamond Books are published by The Berkley Publishing Group,
200 Madison Avenue, New York, New York 10016.
The name "DIAMOND" and its logo are trademarks
belonging to Charter Communications, Inc.

PRINTED IN THE UNITED STATES OF AMERICA

10 9 8 7 6 5 4 3 2 1

TO THE READER

This is a work of fiction. However, certain elements of it are true.

Egbo, the Leopard Society, does exist. No recent outbreaks of the cult have been reported. There is no record of the cult operating in this hemisphere, but who knows for sure?

Vodoun, popularly known as Voodoo, is real. It is one of the most popular and fastest-growing religions in the world.

Tracker is real.

Evildoers, beware.

DYNASTY OF EVIL

1.

"Like I always tell my friends, real life sure beats the movies."

—Ronald Reagan

WHAT WAS THE connection between a blood-cult massacre in the Caribbean and a series of violent deaths in the USA and Europe?

Rory Cobbett, 34, was shot dead by an unknown assailant in a Boston parking lot at night. No witnesses, no suspects, no clues. Police classed it as a botched holdup, although Cobbett's wallet was untouched.

Alana Pershing, 27, fell to her death from the sixth-floor balcony of her fashionable London apartment. Accident, suicide, or murder?

Giselle Durand, 19, was struck and killed by a hit-and-run driver in Paris who was never apprehended.

Helena Carlton, 47, was on board the cabin cruiser *Guinevere* when it went down with all hands in Casco Bay off Portland, Maine. An early-morning fisherman surf-casting on the eastern shore of Peak's Island was the sole witness. He testified that the boat "blew up." Examination of the wreckage that floated to the surface showed that the boat had indeed been destroyed by an explosion. Investigators were unable to determine the cause of the blast. Mechanical mishap or bomb?

Julia Munro, 32, was in the driver's seat when her car went over the edge of a Hudson Valley cliff in New York. The vehicle crashed and burned. Enough remained of the charred corpse for it to be positively identified. Medical examiners found alcohol in her system at a concentration well above the legal definition of drunkenness. She had been commuting home from work at the time of the accident, but police canvassers were unable to find anyone in the bars and restaurants along the route who remembered having served her. The case attracted the attention of certain high-level federal agencies, since the decedent had held a security clearance at the time of her death.

Washington's involvement set off a chain reaction of events that would ultimately rock the Capitol itself. But that final showdown was still in the future.

Belinda Bates-Slawson, 33, was the next to die, hacked to death in a mass slaughter of the occupants of the Slawson's winter home in Port-aux-Frères, on Tambour island in the Caribbean.

Uncle Sam's most unusual sleuth went there.

Blood was everywhere. Dried blood, yes, but no less grisly for that fact. It stained the floor, the walls, even the undersides of the ceiling-fan blades. And that was just the entrance hall of the murder house. There was more blood deeper inside—much more. Seven human beings had died in and around the house.

Four men stood outside the threshold of the open front doorway, looking in. Pierre Martel was captain of the Port-aux-Frères police. Constable Cressy, posted to the hill district above the capital city, had been the first lawman to discover the crime, some sixty hours earlier. Young Jack Lashbrook was the assistant to Wynne Butler, the American consul on the island of Tambour. The Slawsons had been American citizens.

The fourth man was Tracker. He had come from the States to investigate the crime. He was a big man, six-and-a-half feet tall, rangy, long-limbed. He had black hair and copper-colored skin. His profile resembled the face on an Indian-head nickel. He was part Assiniboin Sioux, with red, black, and white ancestors. He wore a short-sleeved safari-style jacket, green T-shirt, loose-fitting khaki pants, and well-worn mocassin-type shoes.

A pair of what looked like visor-shaped dark sunglasses stretched from ear to ear across the front of his face, like a black plastic band. Stark, stylish, ultra-modern, they were the only touch of personal flamboyance about the man.

The late afternoon sunlight was hot, strong, and bright. Tambour was one of the Leeward Islands in the Caribbean Sea, about seventeen degrees north of the Equator. It felt good to be in the shade of the portico overhanging the verandah of the pink chateau on Fire Rock. *Roche de Feu*, the French-speaking islanders called the bench-shaped scarp towering above the capital city on the harbor—Fire Rock. It just as well could have been called Millionaire's Row, for since the days of sailing ships, the masters of the island had made their homes here on the ridge, overlooking the port and an expanse of open sea whose sole boundary was the far horizon. Tambour's great natural beauty and its relative lack of the grinding poverty and brutal crime that afflicted many of the other islands had made it a magnet for wealthy sun worshippers. Their mansions dotted the ridge, favored by cool sea breezes.

Now there was trouble in paradise. Murder was something that happened to the natives, usually on those infrequent occasions when too much rum and a too-handy machete added up into unpremeditated homicide. It wasn't supposed to happen to the rich—but it had. Fire Rock now had the aura of a community under siege. Half the residents had locked up their mansions and left the island, while the other half were forted up in their homes, protected by armed bodyguards and attack dogs.

The pink château would have attracted notice anywhere in the world, but was doubly unexpected amidst the lush green foliage of a tropical isle. It had been built at the turn of the last century by an eccentric exile, the black sheep of an aris-

tocratic family that funded his indulgences on condition that
he never again set foot in France. The structure was a grandi-
ose architectural folly, Gothic-style, complete with gables,
turrets, buttresses, and high arched windows with diamond-
patterned panes. It was made from the pink-tinged stone dug
from the island's quarries, accenting its air of unreality. A
pink mansion with pavilions and gardens, ringed by palms
and mangroves and walls of emerald-green foliage, a vision
out of some wonder-story.

It fronted the interior of the island heights, facing the road
that wound upward from the harbor through the hills to the
top of the ridge. The lowering sun was behind it. A
horseshoe-shaped drive connected the house to the ridge
road. A Land Rover with a blue emergency light mounted on
the roof was parked in the driveway opposite the front entrance.

The foursome was grouped outside the peaked archway of
the front entrance. Shadows were thick in the interior. So
were the flies. Drawn by the blood, they infested the house
like a Biblical plague, humming and buzzing.

Jack Lashbrook caught a whiff from inside. His fine-
featured face screwed up in disgust. He took a quick step
backward.

"Gad! That *smell*!" he said.

"You should have smelled it before the bodies were taken
away," Captain Martel said.

"No, thanks." Shuddering, Lashbrook put a half-dozen
more paces between himself and the door.

Martel was a moon-faced black man, heavy-lidded, with a
natty pencil-thin mustache. The irises of his eyes were yellow, like aged ivory. A stiff-visored commander's cap sat
squarely on his head. His pear-shaped body was uniformed
in a short-sleeved khaki shirt and shorts, knee socks, and
brown shoes. A .9mm pistol was holstered at his right side.
His tailored khakis had razor-sharp creases. His spotless pat-
ent leather visor and gunbelt shone like black mirrors, his
brass gleamed.

Constable Cressy, a giant of a man, seemed to have been
carved from a slab of anthracite. A few inches taller than

Tracker, he was broad-shouldered and deep-chested. His stolid face was all planes and hard edges with professionally neutral eyes. Similarly outfitted to the captain, he toted a shoulder-slung submachine gun in addition to a sidearm.

Officer Jean Baptiste Groux, Martel's driver, stood guard beside the Rover. Two more of Martel's men were posted in back of the mansion.

"Shall we enter, gentlemen?" Martel said, his English slightly accented with a musical lilt, his voice rich and buttery.

"You don't need me to go in with you, do you, Mr. Tracker?" Lashbrook said.

"Not unless you want to."

"This is close enough for me, thanks. I'd just as soon stay out here until you're done."

"Fine."

Consul Butler had assigned his young assistant to serve as Tracker's escort and liasion with the Tambour police for the trip to the murder house.

Martel gestured toward the open doorway. "After you, monsieur."

Tracker crossed the threshold and went inside, Martel following. Cressy stayed outside with Lashbrook.

Flies buzzed their irritation at the intruders. Hordes of them swarmed over the largest of the rust-colored bloodstains.

The entrance hall was part of a long high-ceilinged corridor that spanned the structure from front to rear, allowing cross-ventilation from the sea breezes. The marbled floor had a checkerboard pattern of brown and white squares. To the left, a stairway rose to the second floor. A trail of blood stretched from the foot of the stairs to the middle of the staircase.

"As I reconstruct it from the evidence, Monsieur Tracker, Madame Slawson was just putting her daughter to bed upstairs when the killings started. M. Slawson and the boy were in the den, toward the rear of this floor. Hearing the commotion, Mme. Slawson ran downstairs to see what was happening. She must have reached the far end of the corridor before one of the killers saw her. He struck her with a machete, severing three of the fingers on her right hand as she raised it to protect herself. She turned and ran the other way. He caught her here and struck her down, then kept on hacking until he thought she was dead.

"At that point, the little girl came out of her room and went to the top of the stairs. The killer saw her and started toward her. Mme. Slawson, not yet dead, crawled after him, no doubt trying to stop him. She got as far as the middle of the staircase before he delivered the killing stroke. Then, of course, he killed the little girl," Martel said.

Tracker said nothing. Martel studied the other for some sort of reaction, but the big American's face remained impassive. His eyes were unreadable behind the dark glasses. His head moved slowly from left to right, as if he were scanning the scene, taking it in.

"Mind if I take a look upstairs, Captain?"

"Not at all. My superiors have requested that I extend you every courtesy. Perhaps you will be able to find some clue that I and my men have somehow overlooked."

"I doubt it. You don't strike me as a man who misses much, Captain."

"Monsieur is too kind."

"I'm not here to second-guess your investigation. From what I've seen, it's in fine hands."

"So kind of you to say so. But then, monsieur, if you don't mind my asking—why *are* you here? Washington is a long way off from our little island."

"I have reason to believe that these killings might be related to an investigation that I've been pursuing back in the States. If so, then there's a chance I might be able to throw some light on this crime. Maybe we can help each other out."

"Perhaps. Everything that I've uncovered so far leads me to believe that this is a purely local affair, but I will keep an open mind on the subject."

"I can't ask for more than that."

"Any possible leads you supply will be thoroughly investigated, monsieur. I promise you that."

They went upstairs. Tracker tried not to step in the blood-stains, but there were so many they were difficult to avoid. At the midpoint of the staircase, where Belinda Bates-Slawson had been killed, dull reddish-black droplets splattered the wall as high as the top of Tracker's head.

"The killer must have struck some blow to splash the blood that high."

"Yes," Martel said.

More blood caked the floorboards on the second-floor landing.

"This is where the girl fell. She didn't try to run. She must have been paralyzed with terror, the *pauvre petite*, the poor little one. Remarkable how much blood even a child's body holds, is it not, monsieur?"

An object lay crumpled against the bottom of the balustrade. It was a doll, a baby doll with a bonnet and a lacy jumper, blood-spattered, so that its wide eyes were blinded by dried gore.

Tracker flinched slightly when he noted that pathetic detail, a reaction that was duly noted by Martel. A small sign but a telling one. Despite his almost machine-like exterior, the big American was not totally devoid of human sentiment.

The blood-eyed doll struck a far deeper chord in Tracker than Martel could ever have suspected. Long ago, Tracker's eyes had once been balls of blood, when he suffered the accident that had left him permanently blind.

A drunk driver whose oncoming car had crossed the centerline of the road to cause a head-on collision with Tracker's vehicle had robbed the big man's eyes of their sight. He had survived the crash, but the car had burned and seared the vision from his eyes. Perpetual darkness would have been the fate of any other man, but not Tracker.

Major Nathaniel H. Tracker, United States Air Force, was not in the mode of common men, nor even of uncommon ones. He was a living examplar of the ideal of the Renaissance man: the mind of a genius in the body of a superbly trained athlete. He was one of the new breed of scientist-soldiers who had arisen to meet the challenge of the Space Age. He was an ace jet-fighter pilot, researcher, and inventor. His specialty was the creation and design of instruments that unlocked the secrets of the electromagnetic (EMG) spectrum. He had made significant discoveries in the application of radar, infrared (IR) and ultraviolet (UV) imaging, electro-optics, ultra- and subsonics, laser rangefinders, and motion detectors.

He was more valuable to Uncle Sam at work in the laboratory than aloft in a fighter plane, which had led his USAF bosses to ban him from the aerial combat at which he excelled. Orders were orders and Tracker obeyed them, but there was no stifling the love of adventure that was paramount in the man. Somehow he had a knack for ferreting out evildoers and putting the finish to their careers, and usually their lives, particularly when they threatened the national security of the United States. The Pentagon big brass climbed the walls whenever he was engaged in one of his crusades for fear that a thug's bullet would rob military research and development of one of its greatest scientific wizards. But they had to take it and like it, since any attempt to keep a maverick like Tracker on too short a leash would cause him to rebel and take even greater risks.

After his accident, Tracker had set his great brain to the ultimate challenge of bringing sight to the blind.

Theoretically, it could be done. Many months of intensive thought were required to brainstorm his grand design. The darkness of blindness was lit inside his skull by mental images of columns of equations, schematic circuitry diagrams, cybernetic man-machine interfacings. When his plans were finalized and checked out to the last decimal points, he submitted them to a panel of experts that had been convened by the Pentagon to pass judgment on the feasibility of the scheme.

After much intensive investigation, the experts agreed that it might be possible. Practically, it was another matter entirely. Tracker's trail-blazing video-sonic system was a quantum jump beyond anything that had ever been attempted along those lines. The interface of the proposed electro-optical devices with a human nervous system was a ticklish question. On paper, the system worked, but it had never been tried before on a human subject. Tracker intended to be the guinea pig for the prototype. If his calculations were off, or if unforeseen complications should develop, there was a possibility that the system would literally burn out his brain.

The buck was passed up the line until it came to a stop on the President's desk.

"If Tracker's willing to stake his life on his invention, he's earned the right to do so. This nation certainly owes him that much," the President said.

He knew the full extent of Tracker's secret missions on behalf of the country.

The operation took place under conditions of maximum security in an operating theater at Bethesda Naval Hospital. Everyone present had a top-secret security clearance, from the chief of the surgical team to the humblest orderly. The operation required as much engineering expertise as it did neuro-surgical know-how.

First, Tracker's dead eyes were removed. The insides of his eye sockets were lined with a revolutionary biotic membrane, grown in a vat from a culture of Tracker's own cells to avoid transplant rejection. Micro-miniaturized computer chips were suspended in the membranes, interfacing with the optic nerves that led directly to the brain.

Artificial eyeballs were then implanted. Made from shatterproof ceramic-plastic compounds, they housed miniature video cameras. Irises and pupils were actually focusing lenses. So realistic were the ersatz orbs that only a trained ophthalmologist could tell them from the real thing.

A pair of pinhead-sized holes were drilled into the brow ridges of his eye sockets, then filled with micro-jacks, implants designed to receive the needle-plugs of the exterior eyepiece that would be added later to augment the videosonic system. It had been decided earlier to perform during a single session all surgical procedures needed to adapt the patient to his new cybernetic sensory system. A number of auxiliary operations were done at this time. Among them was the implantation of a micro-transceiver in the bone behind his right ear. The unit contained a mini-microphone able to pick up Tracker's subauditory vocalizations and transmit them as commands to add-on computerized hardware. That is, Tracker's unvoiced whispers could "speak" to computers and computer-guided machinery. An awesome expansion of human mind-power by itself, it was held hostage to the success or failure of the arti-ops in giving eyesight to the blind.

Everything that had to be done was done, and then there was nothing left to do but to turn on the system and see if it worked.

A switch was thrown—and Tracker *saw*!

His vision was like that of no man or woman who ever was. The feed from binocular video camera "eyes" combined into stereoscopic sight, allowing him to perceive objects in depth, three-dimensionally rather than the flat two-dimensional image of a single camera. In many ways, his arti-ops were inferior to natural vision. No mechanism can duplicate the infinite flexibility and versatility of the human eye. But there were compensations.

His video lenses could focus from micro to macro with all stops in between. In his sight he could magnify a blade of grass to the size of a skyscraper or shrink a skyscraper to grass-blade size. Lenticular light-gain boosters let him see in the dark.

An add-on component increased his powers. This was the visor, the curved black eyewear that outwardly resembled a pair of ultra-fashionable sunglasses. In reality it was a complex construction of computerized multi-EMG spectrum sensors. Needle-sized twin jacks protruding on the underside of the visor's upper rim plugged into the corresponding micro-sockets implanted on his brow ridge. The visor was made of wafered polycarbonate, thin and flexible, but tough enough to stop a bullet. Like one-way glass, it let Tracker see out while nobody could see it. Sandwiched between the layers were imaging grids, extending his vision into the infrared and ultraviolet.

Millions of dollars worth of cutting-edge hardware was

wired into his head, but the software was still Tracker, the man himself. Try as he did to buckle down in the lab and perfect his inventions, he couldn't help but get into trouble. Trouble of the killing kind. It was well that he did, for his timely interventions had saved many innocent lives, but adventuring sure played hell with his production schedule.

The Pentagon planners had gotten used to the fact that there was no stopping Tracker from risking his neck on his quixotic campaigns. Indeed, they now monitored his adventures with great interest. Having the prototype sighting system wired into Tracker's skull was the ultimate field test. If the hardware survived Tracker's active lifestyle, it would certainly be able to withstand the rigors of combat, paving the way for a future generation of cyberneticized soldiers.

Only a few people in the highest ranks of the military/ intelligence apparatus knew Tracker's secret: that he was "the spy with the X-ray eyes." Outside the corridors of power, the secret was known by fewer still. Captain Pierre Martel of the Port-aux-Frères police was not one of them.

Martel had been told—*commanded*—to cooperate with Tracker. The order had come from his boss, the District Supervisor, who answered only to the island's governor. *Très bien*, very well, he would cooperate. He would wait for his answers; he was a patient man. Patience is the soul of hunting, especially manhunting.

For now he was content to let Tracker prowl from room to room on the upper floor. He watched Tracker while Tracker looked for . . . what? There was something mechanical, almost robotic, in the slow sweeping motion of Tracker's head whenever he surveyed a room.

Each of the children had had his own room. Windows were shuttered with shades down, untouched since the night of the murders. An adult's room stood next to the girl's, joined by a connecting door.

"The nurse's room," Martel said. "Apparently the little girl was sickly, requiring the services of a live-in nurse. She was not present when the murders were committed."

"Anything in that?"

"I think not, monsieur. It was her weekly night off, and

she stayed overnight at her sister's in town, as was her custom. She is known to me as a person of impeccable reputation. I questioned her extensively and found nothing to contradict that impression. She is not a suspect at this time."

Tracker stuck his head in the nurse's room and looked around. Evening shadows put the space in semidarkness. Martel reached over the other's shoulder and flipped the switch beside the doorway, turning on the lights.

"You will see better with these, M. Tracker."

"Thanks."

"I wonder that you can see at all through those dark glasses."

"Couldn't see at all without them, Captain. Weak eyes. Doctor says that any stray sunlight might inflict permanent damage, especially this bright island sun. So the shades have to stay on."

"Most interesting. You are recovering then from some sort of eye operation, yes?"

"You could say that."

Tracker didn't find anything of interest in the nurse's room so they moved on. Mr. and Mrs. Slawson kept separate bedrooms. That didn't mean anything one way or the other. Her room was perfumed by the sweet scent of lotions, creams, and fragrances. Cosmetics crowded the top of her vanity table. The bed was still made; the spread hadn't been turned down before the slaughter.

Tracker took a closer look at this room, lingering at the writing desk. He started to reach for something on it, then hesitated.

"Yes, monsieur? Something interests you?"

"This magazine—"

"Examine it if you like. Everything has been fingerprinted and photographed, so you need not worry about disturbing the scene. Of course, I would prefer that you keep your handling of the evidence to a minimum."

Sideshow was the name of the magazine, a slick upscale monthly ostensibly devoted to chronicling the latest doings in society and the arts, but which in reality consisted of endless pages of glossy advertisements infrequently interrupted by thin slices of text. The issue was last month's. It lay face-up on the desktop blotter. A piece of paper lay folded inside it, presumably to mark the place where the reader had left off.

Tracker opened the magazine to the appropriate place. The bookmark was a sheet of Belinda Bates-Slawson's personal stationery. It was blank of all writing. It had been placed in the front of the magazine, among the monthly columns, at something called "Peeping Tam," to be exact.

Bylined by one Toby Tam, the column was a gossipy roundup of the recent carryings-on of the trendy international set. Debutantes, models, fashion designers, socialites, and magnates, mostly, with an occasional pop star or screen star thrown in for good measure. A quick scan of the text discovered few names known to him.

Martel was at his shoulder, looking over it at the printed page.

"Does it mean anything to you?"

"Not so far as I can tell. High society's way out of my bailiwick, Captain. The jet set I know does their high-flying in supersonic aircraft, not in nightclubs. Not that I'm knocking nightclubbing, mind you."

"Pity. I confess that I was hoping that you might be able to tie one or more persons named in the column into the case."

"Sorry. But some of them might well have been known to the Slawsons. They moved in similar big-money circles."

"I will run a routine check on every name listed, for the sake of thoroughness, but I doubt we'll develop any new leads from it. Everything so far indicates a purely local origin for the crime, worse luck. Frankly, I would welcome evidence to the contrary, pointing to someone other than an islander as the author of these horrors. It would go a long way in restoring confidence in Tambour as a safe, secure haven for the rich of all nations."

"I can see that a bloodbath like this wouldn't be so hot for the tourist trade."

"To be sure, monsieur, to be sure. Let me add that anyone who can help me toward this goal will have my sincere gratitude."

"I'll see what I can do."

"*Merci*. I can ask no more. Of course, I will welcome evidence of any sort, no matter who it implicates."

"Of course," Tracker said.

His bland agreement caused the other to search his face for signs of sarcasm, but the big American's expression was blank, unreadable.

Tracker examined the sheet of stationery. "Notepaper. Did she plan to write a letter?"

The edge of an envelope jutted out of a wad of correspondence stuffed in a letter rack. Tracker took it from the pile. It was the same color as the piece of notepaper. It was unaddressed, empty.

"Wonder who she planned to write to," he said.

"Who knows?"

"Somebody in the magazine, maybe even somebody in this column?"

Martel shrugged. "An interesting supposition, Monsieur, but tenuous, very tenuous. As thin as air, to be frank. Whereas I now have two suspects locked up in jail awaiting charges, and they are as real as you or I. Known criminals, the pair, with a history of violence. This is fact, not theory."

"Who? Not those sad sacks you showed me back in town!"

"Michel Vachon and Sidiri X, yes."

"Sorry looking mugs. How'd they get all those lumps?"

"Perhaps the arresting officers were a trifle overzealous. Pardonably so, considering the nature of the crime and the circumstances of the arrest. Vachon and Sidiri are bad men, very bad men, not to be taken without a desperate struggle."

"Caught here, weren't they? At the château?"

"On the grounds."

"That was the next night, wasn't it, Captain? The night after the massacre."

"Yes."

"I guess they were the kind of crooks who have to return to the scene of the crime, huh?"

"Apparently."

Martel's mouth was a thin pursed line.

"Pretty big job for just two men. You'd think that at least one of the victims would have got away," Tracker said.

Martel exploded.

"Of course it's not a two-man job! Do you think that I don't know that? Any idiot can see that there were at least four of them, possibly more."

"That's how I read it. I guess that makes me as good as an idiot, at least."

"Your pardon, monsieur. Please forgive my show of temper. This case has put me under a great deal of strain. Also, as the officer in charge of the investigation, I dislike having to admit that some of the culprits are still at large. What man likes to speak of his failures? Not I. It's particularly galling to have to speak of them to a stranger, a foreigner, and—I must be frank, monsieur—an amateur detective who thinks that he will step in and solve the crime after the bumbling police have failed."

Tracker did think something like that, but he kept it to himself.

"Don't mind me. I was just thinking out loud," he said. "I'm finished here. Let's have a look at his room next."

Tracker started for the door. Martel started after him, stopped, paused, then picked up the copy of *Sideshow*. Tucking it under his arm, he followed after Tracker.

W. John Slawson. The "W" stood for Wilmot. His peers called him "Slawson," his underlings called him "Mr. Slawson," and his family and few friends called him "John." Only his mother ever addressed him as "Wilmot." She was eighty-seven and had now outlived him.

Slawson was Old Money who had made plenty of new money on his own. Millions. A businessman who was never far from his work. His bedroom was half office. An attaché case sat on the desktop, its lid open, its insides filled with folders and documents. A week-old folded copy of the *Wall Street Journal* lay nearby, with a pocket calculator set on top of it. There were framed pictures of kids but none of his wife.

Martel said, "M. Slawson was a successful man. Success

breeds enemies. Could his business dealings have had something to do with his death?"

"Massacring the family and everybody else in the house is a bit rugged, even for Wall Street. I'm not saying it hasn't been done, just that it wasn't done here for that reason. It's not about Slawson. The woman is the key."

"Mme. Slawson?" Martel said, surprised.

"Yes."

"M. Tracker, you exasperate me. You are what we call a *provocateur*. Surely you cannot expect your astonishing statement to go unchallenged. If you have information about the case, tell me now!"

"Okay. Back in the States, about ten days ago, a woman went over a cliff in her car and was killed. Her name was Julia Munro and she held a sensitive position in a defense contracting firm. She had access to classified material, some of it highly confidential. Top secret, in fact. When someone like that dies violently, the higher-ups want to know why. Finding out the answer is my job."

"Ah! So, you *are* a U.S. government agent!"

"Not officially. That way, if I screw up they can throw me to the wolves and say I was working on my own."

"Still, you are not without influence. A great deal of pressure must have been applied to the Governor and the District Supervisor to convince them to facilitate your investigation. Ordinarily, they have little use and less liking for foreigners."

"Friends of mine have some clout down here and used it. Unofficially, of course," Tracker said.

"The woman you spoke of, was she murdered?"

"At first Julia Munro's death looked like an accident. Now, I'm not so sure. The forensic evidence is arguable but there's a case to be made for it to be murder disguised to look like an accident. I'll leave that to the experts. I'm no medical man but I know a murder plot when I see one. Some facts I've dug up make it look like murder."

"I see. And what does your one murder have to do with my seven murders, monsieur?"

"Julia Munro and Belinda Bates-Slawson were friends,

good friends. Chums since college days, and before that. They even went to some of the same prep schools."

". . . An interesting coincidence, but perhaps no more than that."

"Oh, no? Well, then, here's the kicker."

Tracker thrust his face forward to emphasize his point. Midnight-blue flecks of light glinted on the dark glasses. For an instant, it seemed to Martel that the light was coming from behind the visor, from Tracker's hidden eyes.

But that was impossible. The blue glints could only have been reflected light bouncing off the lenses, nothing more. Still, it was an unnerving effect. Martel caught himself backing away from the other, a retreat he angrily checked.

"The friendship was current. Julia had a recent letter from Mrs. Slawson. Apparently she was a big one for writing letters. This one told about how she had gone to the funeral of a mutual friend of theirs, a man named Rory Cobbett. I did some checking and found out that Cobbett was a Boston banker who was murdered about a month ago. Shot dead in a botched holdup, according to the official verdict," Tracker said.

"A pattern begins to emerge."

"Now for the kickeroo. They were classmates. Cobbett, Munro, and Slawson all went to the same school, Rockcliffe, a little private college in New England."

"You are on to something, yes—but what? They were murdered because they all attended the same school some fifteen years ago?"

"Could be. That's the only thing they've got in common that I've been able to find so far. I planned to visit the campus for some fact-finding, but I wanted to interview Mrs. Slawson first. When I tried to contact her, I learned that she and her family had just left town on an extended vacation. Not so coincidentally, she left just three days after her friend Julia's fatal 'accident.' She was in such a hurry that she didn't even go to the funeral."

"You think she knew that she was marked for death?"

"I think she was scared and running. The Slawsons usually stayed down here from the third week in December to the first week in January. They've been doing it like that for years. This year, for the first time ever, they arrived before the start of the second week, about eight days ahead of schedule. The sudden departure raised some commotion in the household, but Mrs. Slawson insisted. She was the one who wanted the early getaway. The husband was peeved but afraid that she'd have a nervous breakdown if he didn't give in."

"You seem well-informed on the subject, monsieur."

"It wasn't easy. Prying facts out of the household staff was like getting blood from a stone. They kept mum on their employers' comings and goings, particularly their current whereabouts. I got the impression they'd been told to keep their mouths shut. Lucky for me, the servants next door were nosy and liked to gossip. The local tradespeople didn't mind talking, either. It took plenty of legwork to find out where the Slawsons had gone. By the time I found out, it was too late.

"But I came down anyway, to take a look around and see what I could find."

"Oh? And what have you found, M. Tracker?"

"That I'm more in the dark now than ever!"

2.

MARTEL AND TRACKER went downstairs, then followed the main corridor to the back of the building. Dried bloody footprints trailed across the floor. The end of the corridor branched right and left. Martel turned right; Tracker followed him into a long narrow passageway. The kitchen was at the other end. Midway into the passage, a door opened onto a dining room. Tracker looked inside, seeing nothing of interest.

Martel continued down the hall, stopping a few paces short of the open kitchen doorway. In an alcove to his left, a gray metal panel was mounted on the wall at chest height. About the size and shape of a flooring square, its surface was set flush with the wall. A smaller oblong inside it was a lid or hatch of some sort. It stood a few inches ajar from the rest of the panel. Shiny scratches showed on the keyhole near the right edge.

Martel lifted the lid, exposing an inset instrument panel. There were two vertical rows of switches, with ten switches per column. Each switch had a corresponding light beside it. All the lights were now dark.

"This controls the alarms," he said. "A very advanced system. Motion detectors and electric beams screen the house and grounds to warn of intruders."

"But not on the night of the murders."

"No. For you see, monsieur, the best alarm system in the world will not work unless it is turned on first."

"And this wasn't?"

"No. And now we address one of the most disturbing aspects of the case—disturbing in its implications, which are sinister indeed. Some background is in order. Apparently the household custom was to turn on the alarm after everyone was settled in for the night, masters and servants alike. Otherwise, the alarm would go off whenever anyone stepped outside the house. The servants' quarters are inside the house, in the east wing. Let us say that under ordinary circumstances the alarm would be switched on an hour or so after nightfall. It can only be turned on here, from this panel, which is the master control. M. Slawson handled the nightly chore of turning it on. In his absence, it would be done by the caretaker, Guy, or Simone, the cook. Both were quartered in the east wing. Separate quarters. Guy roomed by himself on the upper floor, while Simone and her daughter shared a room on the ground floor.

"The servants' duties required them to awake at dawn, several hours before their employers rose from their beds. The cool early morning is the best time to do chores. At this time, the alarm would be turned off, by either Guy or Simone, allowing them free movement in or out of the house. I hasten to add that they both were trusted employees of long standing and have spotless reputations. The confidence which M. and Mme. Slawson had in them can be seen in their free and open access to the security system."

"What about the nurse?"

"Nurse Albertine Leclerc's job was to look after the health and welfare of Lori, the young Slawson girl. She would rise about a half-hour earlier than the girl, but well after Guy and Simone. She had nothing to do with the operation of the security system, although she knew the procedure. I learned of it by questioning her."

"Did she look after the boy, too?"

"Phillip was able to take care of himself for the most part. Simone and Guy kept an eye on him to make sure that he didn't get into trouble. From all reports, he was a bright, serious lad, not given to foolish behavior. Mature beyond his twelve years of age."

"Tough break," Tracker said.

Martel shrugged. His shrug and the other's comment meant the same thing.

Tapping the switch-box's lid, he said, "This protective cover locks into place over the controls to prevent their being tampered with. A certain key is needed to unlock it before the alarms can be set. Now, for the sake of convenience, M. Slawson did a careless thing. He kept the key in the lock night and day, around the clock. Doubtless it was handier to keep it in the keyhole than to take it out and put it away whenever it was needed. Especially so, since one or the other of the servants switched off the system in the morning. In effect, the controls were left unsecured. And why not? The servants were trusted members of the household. Why make extra work and risk offending them by going through the constant rigamarole of locking and unlocking the box?

"In other words, the switch-box was locked, but the key was in the lock. It was safely out of reach of the younger children, and Phillip knew enough to leave it alone. It was unlocked and opened to set the controls, to turn the alarm on or off, then it was relocked. The key stayed in the keyhole."

"Convenient."

"Now, there is nothing wrong with this security system, M. Tracker. It is in perfect working order and does exactly what it's supposed to do. It's switched off now, but if I turned it on it would be fully operational. That I will not do, because the presence of my men on the grounds would set off the alarms. But I assure you that it works. That is how Vachon and Sidiri were caught last night. I posted some men on the premises to deter thieves and looters. The alarm system was on. It detected three intruders on the grounds and pinpointed their location. They didn't know that they had been discovered. No alarm was sounded, for the system had been reset earlier to give only silent warning. I had done it in the interests of better thief-taking. Forewarned, my men surprised the prowlers and caught two of them. The third escaped. The two were Vachon and Sidiri."

"What did they want here?"

"They were curious to see the house where the murders had been done, they said."

"That's a good one."

"Unfortunately, we've been unable to persuade them to change their story."

"They must like getting their lumps. Tough guys, eh?"

"Oh, they will soften up soon enough, and then we'll have the truth out of them."

"They must have had a damn good reason for coming back here the night after the murders. You've been working the case, so you must have some pretty good ideas on that score. What's your guess as to why they returned?"

Martel started to say something, stopped, blinked, then began again. "I don't make guesses, monsieur. I am guided by the facts. But that is of no matter. I have let myself be distracted from the fact I was trying to establish, which is this: that the alarm system was and is fully functioning. It worked last night. It would work now if I turned it on. It worked on the night before the murders. I know this because the nurse testified it was so, and because M. Slawson would have called for repairs that day if it had been out of order.

"By all rights, it should have been working on the night of the murders, yet it couldn't have been, according to the evidence. Why?"

"I can make a couple of guesses, Captain. The alarm was sabotaged, put out of commission, then fixed later. Or it was switched off by somebody inside the house. Or, the killers came after dark but before the alarm was turned on."

"I will tell you what happened," Martel said. "When I arrived at the scene of the crime, I found that the alarm system was off, the switch-box was locked, and the key was in the lock. I tried to open it but was unable to do so. The key would not turn the lock. What's more, it was jammed so tightly in the slot that it could not be removed. A pair of pliers in the hands of a strong man was needed to finally free it. The lid had to be pried open with a crowbar. Can you guess why all this had to be done, monsieur?"

"Because it was the wrong key," Tracker said.

"Precisely. It was the wrong key. It must have looked identical to the real one. That would not be difficult, for the key is of an ordinary standard model sold by the thousands in hardware stores. It didn't have to be able to open the lock, only to jam it so that it couldn't be unlocked.

"Here is how I reconstruct the scenario:

"The night before the murders was uneventful. Early that morning, one of the servants unlocked the box, switched off the alarm, relocked it, all part of the daily household routine. Sometime after that, the key was filched and replaced by its double. Later that night, when M. Slawson went to set the alarm, he wouldn't be able to open the box to get at the controls. Not noticing the substitution, he would assume that the jammed key was merely a mechanical mishap. It was too late to call a repairman, for all the shops in town close at sunset. What to do? Go without the alarm for the night and get it fixed in the morning. And I suggest to you, M. Tracker, that that is exactly what was done."

"It doesn't look good for the nurse," Tracker said.

"Eh? Why do you say that?"

"The key exchange. The killers needed somebody on the inside to switch the keys. Only an insider would have known about the setup in the first place. Only an insider could have made the switch. All the insiders are dead, except for the nurse, who just happened to be safely away when the murders went down. It could be coincidence, but the odds are against it."

"Did I mention that the woman is a sixty-five-year-old former nun, who turned to private nursing to support herself a few years ago when her hospital order was closed down due to lack of funds?"

"No, you didn't mention it."

"Neglectful of me. Your pardon, monsieur."

"It does tend to cut down the odds of her being an accomplice. Still, you can never be too sure about what people are capable of doing in a given situation. They can surprise you."

"I begin to warm to you, M. Tracker. Anyone who can consider the possibility that an elderly ex-nun is in league with a gang of killers is a skeptic after my own heart. In an investigation, no one is above suspicion, of course, but in my opinion the possibility of the nurse's involvement in the crime is remote at best."

"If you say so. Trouble is, all the other insiders are dead. I can't see the Slawsons or the servants setting themselves up to be slaughtered along with the rest, even if one of them had a motive for wanting the others dead. Maybe it was planned as a robbery, or pitched that way to one of the insiders to string him or her along. . . ."

Tracker looked thoughtful. "But it wasn't a robbery. It was murder. They came to kill," he said.

"Yes, M. Tracker. They came to kill," Martel said. "But you have overlooked something. The betrayer, the Judas, if you will, need not be a member of the household. It could be a family friend or intimate, even a social acquaintance who was familiar enough with the place to know the particulars about the alarm switch-box."

"And Judas had to be in the house sometime that day to do the key trick. Between dawn and whenever Slawson went to set the alarm that night."

"I agree."

"Hell, Judas could even have been inside *during* the murders! He could have let the killers in and then gone on his way. Or stayed around for the fun."

"A clever scheme, no? Almost diabolical in its understanding of human psychology. If the alarm system showed signs of being tampered with, the family members would have been put on their guard. But a key jammed in a lock is just one of those irritating incidents that people naturally take for granted."

"It would be interesting to know who visited the house that day," Tracker said.

Martel looked around to make sure that no eavesdroppers were about. He saw none. Still, he lowered his voice when he spoke again. "If there were visitors, and I have reason to believe that there were, then the principal witnesses who could identify them are all dead. However, others not directly connected with the scene were in a position to witness comings and goings at the château. Their testimony could lead to a major breakthrough in the case," he said.

"Terrific."

"What I have just told you is to be held in the strictest of confidence. It is not yet common knowledge, not even among my own men. I am relying on your discretion, monsieur."

"You can count on me."

"*Trés bien*, very good. I can tell you now, that even as we speak, my investigators are busy gathering information that will identify all visitors to the château on that fatal day. I expect dramatic developments which will shed an entirely new light on this case."

"You're way ahead of me, Captain. I don't know how you do it."

"That is only to be expected, M. Tracker. After all, you are but an amateur in the game, while I am a seasoned professional!"

The corridor's left branch led into a kind of salon or drawing room. It was high, wide, airy, and spacious. The south wall featured a row of ornate French double doors opening out on a patio. They were curtained with gauzy beige drapes that filtered out much of the intense southern light. Faded heirloom carpets and rugs covered parts of the polished wooden floor. A rugged stone hearth was built into the wall opposite the French doors. There was a lounge, some armchairs, a sofa, and other pieces in various groupings. Massive planters holding man-sized bushes and shrubs filled corners and alcoves.

One of the sets of French doors had been smashed open from the outside. The double doors hung tilting from the hinges at crazy angles. Shards of broken glass were scattered across the floor. Torn curtains. An overturned lamp, its globe shattered but its bulb intact. Fistfuls of shredded upholstery strewn about like thistledown. Blood.

Blood was everywhere. Dried blood. Carpets had soaked up a lot of it and so had the curtains that had fallen to the floor. Black-red splotches were caked onto the exposed

floorboards like scabs. They were in constant motion because of the masses of flies blanketing them.

All walls but the south were decorated with dark wood-
paneled wainscoting. From floor-level to shoulder-height it
was wood paneling; above that, white-painted plastered sur-
faces rose to the ceiling. Above the heavy gray stone slab
mantlepiece that topped the hearth, a message in blood was
scrawled across the wall:

MORTES AUX BLANCS

" 'Death to the whites'—I've still got enough high school
French left in me to translate that," Tracker said.

Martel stood beside him, gazing up at the grisly graffiti.
"Don't be too quick to be fooled by that little calling card,
monsieur. In my opinion, it was put there to deliberately
mislead us," he said.

"A red herring."

"Eh? Red . . . herring? What is that, please?"

"A smelly fish that's used to cover up the scent of the real
trail and lay down a false one."

"Yes, yes, that is exactly what it is. A red herring, indeed!"

"It's supposed to make the murders look political."

"Precisely. M. Tracker, I must speak frankly to you, as
one man of the world to another. Like everywhere else, Tambour has its share of problems. Its history is largely one of
violence and colonial exploitation. It was a major center on
the Caribbean leg of the slave trade and a favorite pirate
haunt. Most of our people are descended from slaves. The island is fortunate for having been largely ignored by the rest
of the world. We are not so peaceful as St. Kitts nor as violent as Haiti or Jamaica.

"For the most part, Tambour folk do not love the rich
whites who settle on the island, nor do they hate them. They
tolerate them for the sake of the jobs they create and the
money they spend, without which life would be just that
much harder. The last thing they want is for the rich to flee

our island and spend their money somewhere else. It would mean economic ruin.

"There is an element of radical extremists who want all whites out, but they are a fringe group, a small but noisy segment of the population. Undoubtedly the militant slogan was drawn on the wall in blood to lay the killings at the radicals' doorstep. And to deter suspicion from the real culprits."

"You don't buy the political angle," Tracker said.

"Like most radicals the world over, the militants' rhetoric is far more violent than their actions. Not that they're not dangerous, a threat to society. They are, but because of that, they are very closely watched. Their movement has more police spies in it than true believers. Infiltrators outnumber extremists two-to-one in the underground cells."

"You've got them covered."

"Monsieur, nothing happens among the rebels but that I don't hear of it first, before their chiefs do. This outrage is none of their doing. It could not be. I would have heard of it first and stopped it from happening, so completely are they monitored. Besides, such butchery is beyond their modest abilities, which are more of the chicken-thieving variety."

"What about your prisoners, Vachon and Sidiri? Are they political?"

Martel shrugged. "Are sharks political?" he said.

He turned, facing south. "It happened sometime between ten and eleven o'clock that night, as far as we can tell. There were six of them. Three came into the house, the others stayed outside. One in the back gardens, another skulking around the house, and a third at the front gate, watching the road.

"Guy the caretaker left the house to walk around outside. He had a flashlight, which was found later near his body. Probably he was making the rounds, making sure that all was well before he retired for the night. A precautionary measure, perhaps, in lieu of the alarm system, which could not be turned on because the lock was stuck. I do not think that he apprehended danger. M. Slawson was a sportsman with a fine collection of hunting rifles and shotguns. None are missing from their places in the gun racks. If Guy feared trouble, he surely would have armed himself, as would M. Slawson. I will return later to the significance of the guns being intact and untouched.

"Exiting by the kitchen door, Guy went around the back of the house, taking a path that runs alongside the west walls. When he was about three-quarters of the way to the front, he must have passed his killer without knowing it. The killer was hiding somewhere in the bushes. The growth is thick, and even though the house lights were lit, there are still many places to hide in. The killer slipped up behind Guy and buried a machete in the back of his head. The blow split his skull down to the eyebrows. He must have died instantly, without a sound. The killer made no attempt to hide the body, although the bushes were only a meter away. The corpse lay on the path where it had fallen.

"Guy's murderer must have signalled to the others that the caretaker was dead. Three came out of hiding in the garden. They crossed the patio to the French doors, smashed them open, and rushed inside. M. Slawson was sitting in a chair, reading, when they burst in. A machete slash partially severed his right arm below the elbow. His legs were cut out from under him.

"The boy, Phillip, was watching television in the den. He ran into the salon, to his death. He suffered multiple stab wounds and slashes, but the killing blow was struck by a different attacker than the one who killed M. Slawson. At some point, Mme. Slawson came downstairs. Her slayer was the one who had not killed yet. The victims suffered multiple attacks, but in all three cases, the killing stroke was struck by a different person. This has been definitely established by the autopsy. The weapons used, the angle and force of the fatal blows, all prove that mother, father, and son were slain by three different persons," Martel said.

"Each of the invaders killed at least one victim. That makes them all equally guilty of murder in the eyes of the law. They might have done it that way deliberately, as a kind of insurance policy. None of them could give up the others to the law without putting his own head in the noose."

Martel nodded. "This is my reading of the ploy, too."

"By the way, do you hang murderers here?"

"No, monsieur."

"You have the death penalty, though."

"Oh, yes. But on Tambour we use the guillotine, not the gallows. You must remember that we used to be a French colony, not a British one."

"The guillotine, eh? I didn't think anybody used that one anymore."

"It is used but rarely here, and then only to execute the most heinous criminals. Under the circumstances, I have no doubt that it will be applied in this case. Murder is bad enough, but child murder demands the most extreme punishment that the law allows."

"Of course, you've got to catch the criminals first."

"I am well aware of that fact, monsieur."

"Who killed the girl?"

"Which one? There were two, M. Tracker. According to the coroner, the man who slew M. Slawson also killed the daughter. Since Slawson was the first to die inside the house, I assume that his killer was the ringleader of the trio. Mme. Slawson's slayer apparently could not bring himself to kill the child at the top of the stairs. The ringleader took care of that.

"Hyacinthe, the cook's daughter, was killed outside by the fifth man, not the one who struck down Guy. Guy's killer and the fifth man killed Simone," Martel said.

"And the sixth? Didn't he kill anybody?"

"No. He was the lookout, posted at the front gate to watch for cars. He was too far away from the house to participate in the killings. There was no way for him to have done so without abandoning his post and thus leaving the others without a sentry."

"He didn't see the murders, so he couldn't testify about who committed them," Tracker said.

"Correct."

"Which makes him the weak link in the chain, if you should ever get your hands on him."

"I already have. It is my belief that Sidiri was the lookout, while Vachon was one of the killers outside the house. I base this on their criminal records, and on their respective natures."

"Could be an angle there, playing one against the other."

"This has been tried, so far without success. They won't talk. They fear their confederates, not the law, despite my efforts to the contrary. Still, I remain optimistic that one or both will eventually break," Martel said.

Tracker walked around the drawing room, eyeing particular points of interest: the writing on the wall, the blood-drenched rugs and furniture, the broken French doors. Mute but eloquent testimony to a nightmare of horror, brutality, and wanton murder. He wasn't a forensics expert, but he was a trained scientific observer. More, he had learned the near-lost art of reading sign and spoor to follow a trail, esoteric woodcraft taught him in boyhood days by his grandfather, a proud full-blooded Sioux.

"Nothing was stolen?" he said.

"Nothing, so far as we can tell. Money, Mme.'s jewelry, watches and other valuables, were all untouched. Which does not rule out the possibility of theft. Something could have been taken, something of which we are unaware."

"But you don't think so."

"Certainly I don't think that robbery was the motive, monsieur. A strong argument against it is the matter of the guns, to which I made mention earlier. M. Slawson had some fine rifles and shotguns in his collection, but no attempt was made to take them. In the islands, guns are more valuable than money, and few thieves could have resisted the temptation to make off with them. The smart ones would know that the weapons would inevitably be traced back to them. Any thief smart enough to know that would also be too smart to be involved with a massacre like this."

"Were any of the victims sexually assaulted?"

"No."

"It wasn't a robbery gone sour. It was murder, nothing but murder. . . . I don't recall your saying anything about gunshots. Were any of the victims shot?" Tracker said.

"No. Stabbed, slashed, choked, beaten, and stomped, but not shot."

"No guns. Interesting. Firearms hard to come by on Tambour?"

"Quite the reverse. There are too many of them in circulation."

"Six killers on a murder mission could've managed to scrape up a few guns between them. But if they had guns along with them that night, they didn't use them. Why? Bullets can be traced, that's one reason. But so can machetes and knives, which they did use. The nearest neighbors are pretty far away. They didn't hear the screams, but maybe they would have heard shots. That could be why guns weren't used. No guns, just blades . . . I wonder if they used blades because they had to?"

"*Had* to? I am afraid I do not follow you, monsieur."

"Doesn't it strike you that there's something ritualistic about the crime? Everyone in the house was killed. They were parceled out so each attacker got at least one kill under his belt, except for the lookout, and he didn't make his quota because he couldn't leave off watching the road. And none of the victims were shot. If it was just plain murder, why not shoot? Shooting's generally more effective and less messy than hacking somebody to bits."

"But not nearly as frightful."

"Right. Terror is part of it, too. Not for the victims, although God knows they must have suffered in their last moments. Terror is for the living. It shows them what to expect if they should run afoul of the killers."

"By that token, it is a warning to *us*, M. Tracker; we who are investigating the crime."

"I can stand it if you can."

"But I am somewhat protected by my position. I have the law behind me, which means the backing of the District Supervisor and, ultimately, the Governor. Killing me would not only be a crime, it would be an affront to those two worthy gentlemen, who would mobilize the power of the state to avenge the insult. Your position, I fear, is not so well secured. Your unofficial status as observer makes you somewhat more expendable. Killing me bears a cost, killing you does not."

"I can stand that, too."

"*Bien, trés bien.* For now, I apprehend no immediate threat to either of us, but in a matter such as this, conditions are liable to change without warning."

"If you're that worried about me, why don't you let me carry a gun?"

Martel's chiding finger wagged like a metronome. "Tut, tut, M. Tracker. We have been over that before. For an outlander to be privy to the details of a homicide investigation is unorthodox enough. To allow you to go about openly armed as you accompany the investigation would provoke too much excitement among the more, er, excitable segment of the population. They have no love for the police and less for armed foreigners."

"Somebody wasn't too crazy about the Slawsons, either."

"A most brutal crime," Martel said. "Those responsible for it will not hesitate to kill again if they feel threatened, or even just to discourage further investigation."

"You trying to scare me, Captain?"

"Not at all, not at all. But I would be remiss in my duties if I did not fully warn you of the risks."

"Thanks. I'll feel much safer sticking close to you, Captain. They won't try to get me while you're around."

"No, they'll wait until I am not around."

"Guess I'd better stick real close to you then. Like glue. Hey, wouldn't it be funny if they knocked you off by accident while trying to get me?"

"How droll, monsieur." Martel's tone implied that it was anything but.

Tracker said, "This is the kind of violence you see in drug killings."

"None of the victims had any involvement with drugs," Martel said flatly.

"No? How about the killers? Or your prisoners?"

"To be a criminal is to be involved with drugs in one way or another, almost without exception. And smuggling is a way of life in the Caribbean. Both suspects have a long history of prior involvement with drugs: Sidiri as a low-level seller, and Vachon primarily as a user. Both are associated with drug gangs. Those gangs are known to us, and none of them, as gangs, are suspected in this case."

"As gangs, you said. Does that mean that some of the members might be involved on their own, as individuals?"

"This is possible, though doubtful. The drug gangs will kill, yes, and as mercilessly as this, to protect their trade. But not a shred of proof exists to even hint that any of the victims, neither family nor servants, had anything to do with the drug trade."

"What about cults?"

"What about them?" Martel said. His face froze, deadpan.

Tracker said, "Drugs and cults go together like ham and eggs. Remember Manson, Jonestown, the Matamoros murders? Some stone outlaw bike clubs in the States use Satanism to keep the membership in line. Jamaican posses use Rasta to do the same thing, Hispanic gangs have Santeria. The cult angle fits right in with the ritualistic nature of the murders."

"And Tambour has . . .?"

"I don't know. You tell me. Voodoo, maybe?"

Martel's laughter was unconvincing.

"M. Tracker, where do you get such ideas?"

"I got that from the tourist guidebook they give out at the hotel. Also from the fact that one of the tours offered by the hotel booking agent is a trip into the jungle to see an authentic voodoo ceremony."

"But that's just for show, a tourist attraction!"

"That's what I thought when I saw that the ticket price also included dinner, drinks, and tips. But that's okay, the tour was cancelled anyway. The hotel guests weren't too keen on going into the jungle, not even with dinner and drinks included. And tips. Not that there were many guests, either. The clerk said that most of them checked out right after the murders. I know the tour package is a phony, pure show business. But don't try to tell me that you can't find the real thing on Tambour!"

"I would not try to tell you anything, monsieur."

"This whole string of islands is known to be one of the biggest centers of the voodoo cult, second only to Haiti!"

"So now you're an anthropologist, too."

"No. But some of the best in the business worked up the background briefing I got on Tambour before leaving the States. They don't guess—they know! And they say that voodoo is alive and well on this island!"

Martel winced. "Actually, the correct term is 'vodoun,' not 'voodoo.' The belief is not uncommon in these parts. But it is a thing of folklore and legend, not the lurid devil's brew of witchcraft and black magic depicted in your Hollywood motion pictures," he said.

"What about the ritual of the Goat Without Horns? That's human sacrifice!"

Martel's wince deepened into a look of pain. "A little knowledge is a dangerous thing, as they say, monsieur. Undoubtedly the practice to which you refer did once exist in the past. Perhaps it lingers on even today, deep in the interior, in the swamps known as the Bayou Roux. But only as a lone act of madness. The evil cult dedicated to such practices was wiped out root and branch many years ago. On this island, at least. Today's vodouniste is most often a respected, law-abiding member of the community. A believer is no more likely to commit murder than your average American churchgoer!"

"I wouldn't touch that line with a ten-foot pole," Tracker said.

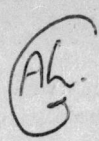

3.

THE CHÂTEAU'S LONG sides ran north-south; its west face was turned to windward. About two hundred yards of ground stood between it and the edge of Fire Ridge, which was more cliff than ridge. Beyond that was empty air and a long, long drop. Thickly wooded foothills sloped down from the bottom of the cliffs to the sea, interrupted at the water's edge by the town of Port-aux-Frères and the harbor.

The sun had dropped below the cliffs but had not yet set. It could not be seen from the patio at the rear of the house, where Tracker and Martel now stood, but its light still filled the sky.

Ornate white-painted wrought-iron lawn furniture, tables and benches and chairs, was grouped on the main pavilion. A series of stepped terraces descended to the ground, which had been landscaped into lush gardens of rainbow-colored flowers and neon-green shrubs. A fountain in a shallow circular pool stood at the center. A broad field had been cleared at the far end of the garden; the grassy weeds were knee-high. The tangled growth of the underbrush hemmed it in, crowding it, trying to reclaim it.

Two of Martel's men, Corporal Bouchard and Auguste Octave, were diligently searching different sections of the garden.

"What are they looking for?" Tracker said.

"Whatever Vachon and Sidiri and the third man were looking for on the night after the murders," Martel said.

"Which is?"

"I do not know, but whatever it is, it must be very important to the killers for them to risk returning to the scene of the crime. They weren't anywhere near the house when they were caught. They were in the gardens, doing what Octave and Bouchard are doing now. They were so intent that it was easy for my men to sneak up on them, though not to take them. The one farthest from the house managed to get into the brush, which was as good as making his escape. You can't find a man in that thicket, especially not at night. But the other two did not escape."

"Didn't they know that the alarm was on?"

"Apparently not. Needless to say, they have not been entirely forthcoming on that subject. Perhaps they thought that the alarm had been permanently disabled, or that they could escape detection as long as they didn't stray too near the house. It must have been something like that; otherwise I doubt that they would have made the attempt. But who knows? Perhaps the object of their search was so important that it was worth the risk no matter what," Martel said.

"That's a puzzler, all right. What could it be?"

"Something that would incontrovertibly tie them to the crime, or something that would unmask the others, possibly even the true conspirators. For now, speculation is as boundless as it is useless. Still, a few generalizations can be made. The object may actually have been lost miles from here, but clearly the killers don't think so. The prisoners didn't find it, for they were still searching when apprehended. It can't be overly large, or my men would have found it in the light of day. I'd have more men searching for it if I could, but I just don't have them. Frankly, my command is already stretched too thin for my liking. Four killers, at least, remain at large—and who knows how many more?"

Flocks of birds crisscrossed the sky, darting into the treetops to roost before the dying of the light. They were noisy: cawing, trilling, whistling, shrilling, shrieking. Fluttering wings beat the air.

"Maybe the others will come back here again to look for what they've lost, maybe even tonight. You could set a trap and bag the whole bunch of them," Tracker said.

"I think not. Things have gone beyond that point. The gang took a severe hit with the capture of Vachon and Sidiri. They must hit back soon to even the score. Their next strike will be more direct, more deadly, I fear. I may well be the next target—or *you*, monsieur."

"It just goes to show you that first impressions are deceiving, eh, Captain? I started out as a bumbling amateur and in a short time I've graduated to being a clay pigeon for a gang of killers. That's what I call progress!"

"You are pleased to joke. That is good. I hope you will be able to retain your oh-so-American sense of humor, come what may."

"I'll die laughing," Tracker said.

Tropical Tambour was a paradise for green growing things. Whatever land hadn't been cleared by the hand of man was overgrown with thick, tangled foliage. Jungle growth bounded the château's grounds, separating it from the neighbors' property on both sides. Green walls fifteen to twenty feet high and as many yards deep, stretched from the cliff's edge to the road, marking off the north and south boundaries of the estate.

The thickets were a mass of trees, vines, creepers, bushes, and shrubs. In some places fallen trees had opened up gaps in the walls, allowing glimpses of the adjoining pieces of property. The mansion on the estate to the north was a good half-mile away from the château, while the house to the south was a quarter-mile distant.

Tracker said, "None of the neighbors heard or saw anything?"

"The folk of Fire Ridge pay a premium for their privacy. They are jealous of their own and generally not inclined to invade that of their neighbors. Both houses are a good distance away. Add to that the isolation imposed by such things as air conditioning, television, radios, and the like, it is not surprising that nothing out of the ordinary was heard by the neighbors during the murders. As to what they or their domestics might have observed prior to the killings that might have some bearing on the case, all I can tell you is that that is a matter which is still under investigation."

"Who are the neighbors, anyway?"

"The north property belongs to Puyter de Groot, a Dutch trader. De Groot is away on business, but Mrs. de Groot— his fourth wife, so I understand—is living in the house with her young son. His older brother, Hans, currently resides there with his family. His stay has been described to me as a visit, but if so it is certainly a lengthy one, for he moved in with his family some eighteen months ago and shows no signs of leaving," Martel said.

He turned, pointing south at a section of house which could be seen through a rift in the trees. The structure was as modern in design as the château was antique, an airy construction of steel, glass, and stone that was set on a slight rise.

"A most unusual construction, that. Modern architecture is rare on Tambour, and rarer still on Fire Ridge, whose wealthy residents are a conservative lot, for the most part. Indeed, they were in an uproar when the fine old house which formerly occupied that spot was torn down so the new one could be raised. But there was nothing they could do about it. The owner held clear title and under our laws was entitled to do what he wanted with the property, so long as it was not a danger to public safety and morals. The owner is a countryman of yours, an M. Leonard Flagler."

Martel searched Tracker's face for a flicker of recognition.

"The name means nothing to you?" he prompted.

"Never heard of him," Tracker said. "Who is he?"

"A banker and financier who has been involved in a number of off-shore investments throughout the island, many of them questionable at best. He is currently under investigation by your SEC, the Securities and Exchange Commission, for multiple counts of stock fraud. But you say that he is unknown to you."

"So many bankers are under investigation back in the

States that it's impossible to keep track of them all. Anyhow, stocks and bonds are outside my bailiwick."

"What in fact is your . . . ah . . . bailiwick . . . M. Tracker?"

"National security and defense technology."

"M. or Mme. Slawson were involved in such things?"

"Not to my knowledge. Like I said, all I've found out is that Mrs. Slawson knew Julia Munro, whose death I'm investigating. They were friends, and they both died violent deaths within a few weeks of each other. . . . But this Owen Flagler interests me. So does de Groot, for that matter."

"And myself as well. For a time, I half-suspected that Flagler might have been the intended victim, and that the Slawsons were slain by mistake. Flagler's murky dealings in international bank fraud supply an excellent motive for murder. But the business with the alarm box key destroys that theory. It proves that the château had to be the target from the start."

"How did Flagler and Slawson get along?"

"They were social acquaintances, and nothing more than that, so far as I can tell. At that, I would say that Slawson got along better with Flagler than de Groot did. Slawson acquired his property five years ago, long after Flagler put up his modernistic house. De Groot was an owner well before Flagler came on the scene. Indeed, his wife was one of the leaders of the drive to stop Flagler from building his house of glass."

"How did de Groot get along with Slawson?"

"Amicably enough. At any rate, the police have never been called to adjudicate a dispute between any of the parties. Not that there was much interaction between the three. Slawson was a seasonal resident, staying here for a few weeks at a time, several times a year. De Groot is a year-round resident, but is often away for months at a time, such as now. But some of his family is always on the premises. Flagler stayed here for a year or so, after the place was first built, then began absenting himself for longer and longer periods of time. In the last year he has been here only once or twice, and then for very short stays. Perhaps this has something to do with his legal troubles, or perhaps not. His adult daughter, Mlle. Kirsten, has lived in the house for the last two years. He is regarded as money-mad and is at best tolerated, but she is widely liked and admired. A most extraordinary young woman . . ."

"How so?"

"She is well-respected for her many charitable works on behalf of the poor, particularly the children. Not content merely to sign checks, she takes an active role in the welfare of the people."

"A do-gooder, eh?"

"You say that as if it was somehow discreditable, M. Tracker."

"Not at all. I'm a do-gooder myself."

"Mlle. Flagler is also something of a scholar. She has made herself most knowledgeable about the history and customs of Tambour. She has published a number of monographs about our folkways."

"Maybe I should have a talk with her."

". . . I think not. After all, monsieur, if you are a target, and there is every possibility that you are, you must be extremely careful of your associations, since anyone you are seen talking to might also attract the attention of the killers. Tambour cannot afford to have anything happen to Mlle. Flagler."

"No, just to me, huh? Don't answer that, I know the answer already."

"In fact, I must insist that you speak to no principals in the case without consulting me first."

"That puts a cramp in my investigation, Captain."

"But not mine. The waters are murky enough without you muddying them further. I remind you that you are a guest in Tambour, and my guest on this investigation, which is the only investigation that interests me."

"Well, then, maybe you could arrange it for me to interview some of the people you've mentioned."

"This is possible, but not a priority. Something along these lines might well be arranged, however."

"Okay for me to take a look around the grounds, or is that out of bounds, too?"

"Certainly not! Look as much as you like. That is why you are here. But please, no wandering off where I or one of my men cannot see you at all times. That would be . . . imprudent."

"Right," Tracker said.

He went down the stairs at the west side of the pavilion and walked around on the grassy ground between the short, south face of the house and the jungle wall at the property's edge.

A torn-up piece of turf lay about a stone's throw away from a side door, the only exit on the south side of the house.

"Simone Tonnelle and her daughter, Hyacinthe, fled through that door, trying to escape. They were caught in the open by the two killers posted outside the house. They did not escape," Martel said. He had been following at a discreet distance but now was abreast of him.

Blood stained the grass brown.

"It is my belief that Vachon was one of the outside men, and that Sidiri was the lookout at the gate."

"I thought you didn't make guesses, Captain."

"That's not a guess, it is a hypothesis based on fact. Sidiri is a cunning rogue, to whom murder is a last resort. He is not squeamish, but prefers to leave the rough stuff to those who have a taste for it. Vachon is a much more violent individual, an associate of some of the crudest and most brutal criminals on the island. He comes from the shantytown in Elysée des Cendres, 'Ashfield' to you, a low place that has spawned some of our most dangerous criminals.

"The job of lookout would have been much to Sidiri's taste, particularly if he was well-paid. Vachon is a killer, stubborn but not too smart. I doubt that he would be trusted to do the work inside the house; but outside, as a backup man—yes," Martel said.

"So Vachon killed the cook and her little girl?"

"He and the other outside man, the one who struck down Guy. To put an even finer point on it, I believe that that man was the senior partner of the two, senior in authority, that is, since he had the more important job of disposing of the care-taker. Vachon is a follower, not a leader."

Tracker turned, focusing his attention on the gardens. The flower beds were a riot of color: orange, lemon-yellow, lime-green, midnight-blue, violet, vermilion, purple-black. The heavy floral scents were rich, intoxicating. Winding paths honeycombed the garden plots. Tracker began wandering them, seemingly at random.

Octave and Bouchard looked up from what they were doing to watch him, returning to their tasks after a moment when it became apparent that Tracker was making the rounds to no purpose. Martel reached the same conclusion and stopped trying to keep up with Tracker but instead let him go where he pleased unescorted, as long as he stayed within bounds.

Tracker drifted to the center of the landscaped area, paus-ing at the fountain, which was turned off. The still water in the round shallow reflecting pool was stagnating, its surface streaked with streamers of pale green scum.

He repeated the motion which had unscttlcd Martel earlier, that slow deliberate turning of the head to pan his gaze across the landscape. Facing west, his gaze swept across one hundred eighty degrees of landscape, from ex-treme left to right. He turned, facing the château, and did the same thing, not stopping until he had surveyed the other half of his surroundings.

Something in his intent attitude reminded Martel of a hunting dog quivering on point. All except for the dark vi-sored sunshades. There was something suggestively insectoid about them, like the oversized eyes of a fly, or more accurately, a praying mantis.

Completing his survey, Tracker once more ambled through the gardens. Rounding the central plaza, he started back toward the house.

Footsteps sounded on the flagstones behind Martel, who was standing on the pavement trying to puzzle out what Tracker was up to. Glancing over his shoulder, he saw Con-stable Cressy approaching.

Cressy halted alongside him, started to speak, then

screwed up his face into a frown as he saw Tracker crossing the white-pebbled path at the head of the garden.

". . . What is he doing, sir?" he said, low-voiced.

"I don't know. I don't even know if *he* knows. . . . But was there something you wanted to tell me, Cressy?"

"I just wanted to find out our schedule, sir. It will be dark soon."

"Yes."

"It is a long way back to town. It would be well if you were back there before the sun goes down."

"Don't tell me that a big fellow like you is afraid of the dark!"

This was said in a bantering tone, since Martel knew that Cressy was so careless of his personal safety that he would charge into a lion's den if the lion in question were wanted by the law.

"I am afraid, Captain, afraid for you. There are many places on the road where ambushers could hide, especially at night."

"Attack me? They wouldn't dare!"

"Why not? With you gone, there would be no investigation, and the killers would be able to cheat justice."

"Never, so long as you are on the case, Cressy."

"But I would be dead, too, for they would have to kill me first before they could get to you."

This was no self-serving statement meant to curry favor with his chief; it was a simple statement of fact, and Martel recognized it as such. That was Cressy: simple, direct, uncompromising.

"Good man," Martel said. "Then we must both stay alive. Otherwise, who will show our American colleague the way back to his hotel?"

Cressy's sly grin showed that his chief's little jest had not gone unappreciated.

The pathway on which Tracker now trod ran parallel to the house's long sides, stretching lengthwise between the pavilion and the near edge of the gardens. The deck of the pavilion was raised five feet above the ground. A wide stone staircase descended from the middle of the platform's long west side; two smaller sets of steps slanted down from either of the short sides.

Tracker stood on the path between the stairs and the pavilion's northwest corner, with only his head and shoulders showing above the top of the deck.

"Hey, I think I found something."

"Yes, M. Tracker? And what is that that you think you have found?" Martel said. He had to fight to force some polite interest into his reply, and was not entirely successful in doing so.

"Maybe you better come over and take a look at it. Could be evidence!"

"To be sure, monsieur, to be sure."

Martel, sighing, flashed Cressy one of those see-what-I-have-to-put-up-with? faces, before crossing to the far edge of the pavilion.

Tracker was pointing toward the base of the wall, which was lapped by an ankle-high tangle of greenery.

"See it?" he said.

"No, monsieur, I see nothing but some weeds in need of trimming, and I have seen them before, thank you very much—"

Martel had been speaking with some stiffness, so that even this obtuse American would realize that he did not suffer fools gladly, but he shut up in mid-sentence when something unexpected caught his eye.

Dropping to one knee at the platform's edge, he peered straight down at the place indicated by Tracker. Frowning, eyes narrowed, he perceived the vague outline of some unknown object all but hidden by the weeds.

"What—? By heaven, I do believe you're right. There is something there!"

Turning his back on his discovery, Tracker went to a marble bench a dozen paces away. A long-handled garden rake lay on the ground beside it. Tracker picked it up and returned to his previous position on the path.

By now, Cressy stood alongside Martel, while Octave and Bouchard craned to see what all the fuss was about.

Holding the rake in both hands, Tracker dipped the comb

into the scrub at the base of the wall. Pulling a mass of broad-leaved weeds toward himself, flattening them against the ground, he exposed a narrow drainage ditch, about six inches deep, that bordered the bottom of the wall.

Something was in that hidden ditch. Tracker scooped it up in the tines of the rake and brought it to light.

A skeletal black object, long, angular, and spiky, it superficially resembled a hand-held gardening tool, one that had been misplaced and forgotten and left to rust a long, long time ago.

Measuring less than twelve inches long, it consisted of a stem-like handle with three wickedly curved hooked prongs at one end. Suggesting the talons of some great beast of prey, reaching out to slash and tear, it was made of age-blackened iron, pitted with corrosion. The stains on the prongs could have been rust. Whatever they were, they were old, ancient. A thin metal ring jutted from the pommel, trailing a rawhide thong of far more recent vintage. One end of the thong was still knotted to the ring, while the other end hung free.

"What do you suppose that is?" Tracker said.

Martel blinked rapidly, his yellowed eyes staring. Cressy was utterly without expression, except for a nervous tic that kept firing in the corner of his left eye.

The other two gendarmes had come closer for a better look. They got one.

Octave grunted, as if elbowed in the stomach.

Bouchard stepped backward, reeling, holding his hands palms outward at shoulder height. *"Egbo!"* he shouted, gasping.

4.

TRACKER KEPT ON displaying his find. He was nonchalant, pleasant-faced, seemingly unaware of the effect produced by the discovery.

"You sound like you know what this is," he said to Bouchard.

He turned toward the corporal of police, swinging the rake with its prize toward him. Bouchard squawked, twisting to one side to avoid contact with the thing.

Octave stood with fists at his sides, muscles tensed so tightly that he shook with the strain.

"The way you guys act, you'd think it was poison or something," Tracker said.

Martel finally found his voice. He was pleased to note that it betrayed not a tremor of unease. "Not poison—*dynamite*," he said.

"Hot stuff, eh?"

"M. Tracker, do not touch the claw. Leave it exactly where it is until I can take possession of it. I repeat, do-not-touch-it."

"That's why I used the rake to pick it up. Maybe you'll be able to find some fingerprints on it," Tracker said.

Martel went down the stairs to the garden with Cressy right beside him.

"Think this is what your killers were looking for, Captain?" Tracker said.

"There can be no doubt about it. But how did you of all people manage to find it when no one else could?"

"Because he is a witch!" Bouchard blurted out.

"Now, now, Corporal—"

"It's true, Captain! That must be why he keeps his eyes hidden, because he has the Evil Eye!"

"Bouchard! Take hold of yourself, man! You're talking like a superstitious fool, not an officer of the law. Remember the uniform that you wear!"

"I—yes, you are right, of course, my captain. Please excuse my outburst."

"We've got to keep our heads at a time like this or risk losing them. Although I admit that finding the claw is enough to unnerve anyone."

"How about letting me in on the secret, Captain?"

"All in good time, monsieur. First you must tell me how you found it."

"Call it beginner's luck."

Martel shook his head. "That is not good enough."

"I figured that anybody sneaking up on the house from back here would use the pavilion to cover their approach. They could come up to the edge of it and look over the top. That way they'd be able to spy on the house, keep close tabs on it without showing more than their heads. So I focused on that area, not looking for anything in particular, just looking hard. Plus, I remembered that you said you caught the prisoners farther away from the house, so that was something else that pointed me here. I made a lucky guess and I got lucky," Tracker said.

Martel didn't bother to hide his skepticism.

"Such good fortune seems little short of miraculous, monsieur."

"The Lord moves in mysterious ways, or so they say."

"Yes, but you are not the Lord. You are not even a citizen of our fair isle. Any fair-minded man would have great difficulty in believing that you just 'happened' across this vital clue by sheer chance. One might almost be tempted into thinking that you played a more active part in the discovery, by placing it there yourself."

"How? You've been with me the whole time, ever since we left town. Where was I supposed to be carrying the damned thing, in my hip pocket? It would have stuck out a country mile!"

"I did not say that I thought you had planted the evidence, I said that it was tempting to believe that you had."

"Why would I do that? Just to pull a fast one on you for the fun of it? I've never been here before, and I don't know anybody on Tambour from Adam. I'll go when my job is done and the sooner that is, the better, meaning no disrespect to you or your island. In the meantime, this is the thanks I get for turning up an important piece of evidence. Hell, I don't even know what the damned thing is!"

" 'Damned thing' is the most apt description for the claw."

"If you want it, take it, whatever it is. I'm getting tired of holding it up on the end of this rake."

"Gladly, monsieur. Now that you have vented your little blast of temperament, we will proceed to business. If you will be so good as to hold it for a moment longer, so that it can be properly received as evidence . . ."

"Sure."

"Thank you," Martel said. He looked at each of his men in turn, but whatever he was looking for, he didn't find it.

"Where is the evidence kit?" he said at last.

"In the car, *mon capitain*."

"What's it doing there, Bouchard?"

Bouchard held his hands out from his sides. "Who knew there would be new evidence? Especially, evidence like this . . ."

Glancing at the claw, Bouchard shuddered.

"Get the evidence kit, fool!"

"I'll get it, Captain," Octave said.

"Then do so, and be quick about it!"

"Yes, sir. I'll cut through the house instead of going around it to save time."

"Don't talk about it, do it!"

"Sir!"

Octave flashed a salute, turned, climbed the stone stairs, and double-timed across the pavilion. As he ran he held his holstered gun to his side to keep it from flopping about. He disappeared inside the house.

Noise erupted as a mass of multi-colored birds suddenly took wing, all at once, deserting a treetop perch. The tree they had abandoned was somewhere in the north clump of woods, about midway between the edge of the cliff and the pavilion. Raucous, indignant, the scattered birds settled on other nearby perches.

Bouchard had started at the disturbance, and Martel, frozen-faced, had clapped his hand to his gun. Cressy looked thoughtful.

Tracker adroitly maneuvered the rake so the claw became caught between the tines. That allowed him to stand the rake upright, with the butt resting on the ground and the claw clutched tight in the comb.

"That's better. My arms were getting tired. Claw, eh? It looks it. Nasty piece of work. What is it, the local equivalent of brass knuckles or something?" he said.

"It is evil!" Bouchard said.

"Old, anyway. Iron hasn't been forged and worked like this for the last few hundred years. This is a real antique," Tracker said.

Martel and Cressy bobbed their heads, peering at the artifact from different angles.

"How the masked priest must have raged when this was lost!" Martel said.

Cressy nodded his solemn agreement.

"No wonder they came back, Cressy. They had to!"

"Yes, Captain, and the others will keep coming after it until they get it, or they are destroyed."

"What is it, Captain, some kind of voodoo talisman?"

"A talisman, yes, but sacred to something far more dangerous than vodoun, monsieur."

"Which is . . ."

"Egbo!"

It sounded like a nonsense word to Tracker, but just hearing it spoken made Bouchard groan aloud.

Purple shadows had been steadily advancing across the grounds as the sun lowered. The investigators were too absorbed in the find to take much notice of the passing of the light. Now, long slanting shadows began to roll over them.

Cressy, fretting, stared into the western sky to estimate how much more daylight was left to them. Not much. Dusk is short and night falls fast in the tropics.

"Eee-go-bo? What's that?"

"Not eee-go-bo, monsieur. *Egbo*," Martel said.

He was watching Bouchard as he spoke, and this time the corporal was careful not to react.

"*Egbo* . . . I've never heard the word before."

"For which you should be profoundly grateful, M. Tracker."

"It's not French, is it, Captain?"

"No. It is of West African origin. A very old word to describe an ancient evil."

"What, the claw?"

"The claw is not *Egbo*, but it is sacred to the *Egbo*. I was not joking when I said that the claw is dynamite. It could blow this case wide open. It could also blow up in our faces. I will not lie to you. Finding the claw has put us all at extreme risk," Martel said.

Another disturbance, as birds once more evacuated *en masse* from their roost in the leafy green canopy atop the north thicket. The site of the disruption was somewhere between the far end of the garden and the central plaza, deep in the brush. Appreciably closer than the first such incident minutes ago. Twilight rendered the impenetrable tangle of woods still more opaque.

"Perhaps a cat is among the birds," Cressy said.

"Let's hope not," Martel said.

"Octave is a long time returning," Bouchard said. His fingers fiddled with the snapped-down flap of his holstered gun.

The gendarmes watched the house. A few more minutes ticked past, with still no sign of Octave.

"What's keeping him?" Bouchard said.

"The evidence kit couldn't have been forgotten back at headquarters, could it?"

"Certainly, not, *mon capitaine*! I myself loaded it in the car before we left!"

"It was on the floor of the front seat on the passenger side," Cressy said.

"So? Well, we will do what we can to save time. I prefer not to linger here overlong," Martel said. He pulled a handkerchief from his breast pocket, unfolding it with a deft flick of the wrist. Holding the white linen square in one hand, he wrapped it around the pommel of the claw and freed it from the rake. Careful not to touch it with his bare hands, he put the claw in the cloth and knotted the four corners together, making a kind of linen carrying bag. Holding it by the knotted top, he could move it without damaging whatever fingerprints had been left on it, if any. "Now that the evidence has been properly secured, after a fashion, we need delay our departure no longer," he said.

Martel started toward the house. Taking their cue from him, the others did the same.

"I am far from satisfied with your explanation as to how you found the claw. We will take up the matter again, later," Martel said.

Tracker shrugged. "You never did get around to telling me what *Egbo* means."

"*Egbo* is a secret society, the murderous cult of the—"

Martel was interrupted by gunfire.

A muffled shot sounded, seeming to come from the front of the house. An agonized cry followed, only to be silenced a heartbeat or two later by a second shot, which rang out loud and clear compared to the first.

Bouchard was first to react, snaking his gun out of the holster in a lightning-like blur of motion and rushing the house.

Cressy drew his gun, too, crossing the pavilion at an angle toward a different set of doors than those that Bouchard had just gone through.

Transferring the bag with the claw to his left hand, Martel drew his pistol and started after the others.

"Everybody's got a gun but me!" Tracker said.

"You will not need one so long as you are careful to stay close to me! *Allons*, let's go, hurry, *vite*, *vite!*"

"I'm right behind you!"

Cressy stood just inside the doorway, motioning to Martel that the way was clear. Footsteps slapped the flagstones as Tracker and Martel raced to the door and through it.

Bouchard ran down the long main corridor toward the front of the house. The big front door was open wide. Nearing the arched entryway, he veered to one side, removing himself from the line of fire if any shots came blasting through the portal. Apart from the evasive move, he did not slacken his headlong pace one iota.

The floor was slippery and he almost fell while trying to come to a stop. He hit the wall to the left of the doorway, taking the blow on his shoulder to absorb the impact. He bounced off it, staggered, recovered.

There had been no more shooting since the first two shots. Back to the wall, Bouchard edged to the doorway, ducked low, and charged through it, half-expecting a bullet to come crashing into him.

Gun leveled, he crouched on the verandah, trying to see everywhere at once. Motion flashed in the corner of his left eye, and he wheeled to face it, swinging the gun into line.

"Don't shoot!"

Jack Lashbrook huddled against a column, raising his hands to show that they were empty. He was afraid, near panic. And no threat, Bouchard decided in a flash. The young consular assistant was innocent of the shooting.

A body lay flat on the grass on the other side of the driveway. Farther down the drive, almost at the edge of the property, the police car was fleeing the scene. Gears grinding, tires squealing, the car whipped through the main gate, made a hard right onto the road, then bulleted down the straightaway until it was lost from sight.

Cressy and Martel spilled out onto the verandah. Gun pointed at the body in the grass, Bouchard darted across the driveway toward it. He was hunched low to present less of a target.

The body of a gendarme lay sprawling on its back, arms extended from its sides. It had been shot once in the stomach and once in the head. The stomach wound was bad enough, but the head shot was a gory mess. It had sheared off the top of the skull and taken most of the brain with it. The head wound had already spilled a bucket of blood and was still going strong.

Dashing up alongside Bouchard, Martel stopped short within a few inches of the corpse.

"Who—?"

"It's Groux, your driver, *mon capitaine*!" said Bouchard.

"And Octave? What of him?"

"I'm not sure, but I think that was him who just drove away in our car!"

"What deviltry is this?"

"This one can give us some answers," Cressy said. He held Lashbrook's arm above the elbow, steadying him as he steered him toward the others. Lashbrook sagged at the knees as he neared the body.

"No, please, I can't bear to see it!"

"That's close enough," Martel said.

Cressy nodded, halting in the driveway a half-dozen dozen paces from the dead man. Lashbrook turned his face away from the grisly sight, leaning on Cressy for support. He would have fallen without the help of the constable's bracing hand.

"What happened?"

"You've got to believe me, Captain, I had nothing to do with it! I swear!"

"I believe you, M. Lashbrook. Now get a grip on yourself and tell me what has happened here."

"I—well, there's not much to tell, not really. That's what's so crazy about it. There wasn't any warning, it just happened. I was sitting outside waiting for you to finish. One of your men came out—Octave, I think his name is, I don't know if that's his first name or his last—"

"Yes, yes, Octave. Please go on."

"There wasn't much to it. He went to the car and said something to your driver, I couldn't hear what it was. He wasn't angry or anything like that. I didn't think anything of it and was barely paying attention. Then Octave opened the door and got behind the wheel. The driver didn't like that. It looked to me like he was telling Octave to get out of the car. He started yelling and opened the door.

"Then there was a shot. At first I thought it was a backfire from the car being started up. But it wasn't. The driver doubled over and grabbed his stomach like he'd been shot there. He fell down. Octave got out of the car and stood over him and shot him again. Then he got back in the car and drove away.

"It was all so fast that I didn't even know what happened until it was all over. I didn't think to move until the car was halfway down the drive. Then I ducked behind a pillar and stayed there until you showed up. That's all I know about it, I swear!"

"Please, M. Lashbrook, control yourself."

"I can't. Look at me, I'm shaking like a leaf. That's the damnedest thing I ever saw. He killed that man in cold blood, just shot him dead with no more emotion than if he was stepping on a bug! Murdered him for no reason!"

"He had a reason, a very good reason for doing what he did."

"For God's sake, what?"

"It is very simple, monsieur. Octave needed the car. Groux tried to stop him from taking it, so Octave killed him. He shot Groux once, then, being a methodical man, made sure to deliver the *coup de grâce*. But the murder was only incidental to the theft of the car."

"One cop blows away another cop so he can steal a police car? That's even more insane!"

"On the contrary. By stealing the car, Octave has succeeded in his plan."

"What plan?"

"To leave us here without a car," Martel said.

It took a few seconds for that one to sink in.

"Huh? Why would he want to do that?"

"You don't look at all well, monsieur. I suggest that you

sit down and rest for a few minutes until you feel better. See to it, constable."

"Yes, Captain."

Still holding Lashbrook by the arm, Cressy escorted him to a white wrought-iron bench on the verandah, sidelining him. Lashbrook was stunned, shocked, scared.

Bouchard stood beside Martel in the drive. "Groux's holster flap is still fastened. That swine Octave never gave him a chance," he said.

"Forget his chances and start worrying about your own."

"Think we're in for a fight, Captain?"

"The fight of our lives, Bouchard."

"Because of . . . the claw?"

"Yes."

"Good. Let them come. They'll pay in blood for their little bauble!" Bouchard shook his fist.

"You seem to have gotten over your fear of the *Egbo*, Corporal."

"It's like this, sir: I was afraid of them, for reasons you know only too well, having gone up against them before. But when I saw poor Groux lying there, treacherously killed by a comrade he trusted, I stopped being scared and got mad."

"Good man! Stay that way and you just might get out of this alive. I—" Struck by a sudden thought, Martel fell silent. With intent, searching gaze, he made a quick scan of the scene but failed to find what he was looking for.

"Something is wrong, *mon capitaine*?"

"Bouchard! *Where is Tracker?*"

"I don't know, I thought he was with you, Captain."

"He was, but he's not here now. Where did he go?"

"He must be around here someplace," Bouchard said. "After all, a man can't just vanish into thin air . . . although with that one, I'm not so sure!"

5.

FINDING THINGS IS easy when you've got a few million dollars worth of high-tech hardware wired into your head.

Finding the claw had been especially easy because it was made of metal, although Tracker hadn't known that when he first started looking for it. All he'd known was what Captain Martel had told him, that the killers had returned to the scene the night after the murders. That, and the well-grounded hunch that it must have been something pretty damned important to tempt them into making that risky return.

When Tracker had gone into the gardens where the prisoners had been caught, the odds were that whatever they were looking for had probably been lost in that area. So Tracker put his own sophisticated search system to work.

Standing at the southeast corner of the landscaped grounds, at a place where he could bring the entire area under his gaze, he switched over to cybernetic search mode.

Had any of the gendarmes looked him over carefully at that moment, they might have noticed that he seemed to be talking to himself. His lips moved, though no sounds came forth. He *was* talking to himself, in a way that no one but the initiated could comprehend.

A minor sub-process of the massive experimental surgery he had undergone at Bethesda had been the insertion of a microscopic audio transceiver into the bone of his skull an inch behind his right ear. No bigger than the head of a pin, the implanted "bone phone" enabled him to verbally command the array of computer optics in his eyes and visor. Part of the implant was a receiver set to pick up his sub-auditory vocalizations. When he wanted to program a command into the system, he would speak the words without audibly vocalizing them. The receiver picked up the movements and vibrations of his voicebox, translating them into coded electrical impulses. Before inputting a command, Tracker had to give certain passwords, alerting the receiver that he was initiating command functions. This precaution ensured that ordinary spoken words would not be mistaken for commands, so he wouldn't have to worry about inadvertantly triggering an opti-computer function.

The other half of the implant transmitted the electrically coded voice commands to the control processing unit in his computerized visor, which would then initiate the requested function.

Simply put, when Tracker seemed to be mumbling something under his breath as he stood at the edge of the garden, he was really voice-activating a search program in his computer optics.

Many such processes were his to command, but he started off with a pulsed metal-detecting sweep of the area. Twin micro-miniaturized wave generators had been placed opposite each other, one in each corner of the top rim of his visor where the earpieces met the frame of the lenses.

They began pulsing, sending out ever-widening spherical electromagnetic waves. The energy waves were not unlike the ripples created when a stone is dropped into a pond. As each of the twinned wave-pulses expanded, they intersected one another in an intricate crosscross pattern. Any metal object that lay in the intersection of those two fields would show up as a blip on Tracker's screens.

The screens were fused into the layered polycarbonate visor. There were different screens for different functions, a multiple array allowed by the micro-thinness of the overlaid imaging grids sandwiched one atop another in the composite lenses. The images were seen superimposed over Tracker's video vision, ghostly holograms depicting sections of the EMG-spectrum invisible to the naked eye. The one-way tinting on the outside of the visor prevented anyone from seeing what Tracker saw on the inside of the lenses. The outer shield was not completely opaque, accounting for the glints and flashes of light that observers sometimes noticed in the visor, as Captain Martel had earlier.

Tracker slowly panned his visored gaze from left to right, systematically sweeping the garden grounds with his built-in metal detector. The process was simply a refinement of the metal detectors used to screen passengers prior to entering the boarding gates of airports.

Search parameters were established. There was no sense in wasting time on objects that were too small or too big. As the wave-pulses scanned the surroundings, metal objects appeared as bright spots on the inner lens screen. The more metal, the brighter the image. The objects didn't have to be out in the open to be seen. The metal detector saw through such things as leaves, grass, dirt, and non-metallic items that were opaque to the human eye.

A parade of objects flitted across his screens: the rusted tip of a broken garden tool, a child's toy truck, a horseshoe, a pair of dead flashlight batteries, a coiled spring, a scattering of lost coins of different currencies, all the debris and detritus that can accummulate in a large outdoor space, even a well-maintained one such as the gardens of the pink château.

A ghostly parallel world existed below the surface, for the metal detectors could "see" a few feet deep into the earth. There were webs of cables for the electric lights and the motion-detecting alarm sensors; a phantom gridwork of pipes, valves, and pumps existed to supply water to the fountain and the sprinkler nozzles studding the flower beds.

When a particular object piqued his eye, Tracker tagged it and zoomed in for further identification, thanks to his voice command system. His vision was capable of narrowing in on a microscopic level or expanding to telescopic magnitude. He could shrink an image or magnify it at will, or even log it into the hardware's computer memory for later study.

Room-temperature superconductive circuitry allowed the

intricate hardware to do so much and yet use so little power. The power source was Tracker's own body heat, which the system's convertor cells transformed into electrical energy. The incredible efficiency of superconductive circuitry maximized the effect of this steady power source. A pair of coin-sized refrigeration units embedded in the thickest parts of the earpieces served as added protection against the hardware overheating.

Tracker didn't know what he was looking for, exactly, but he had a few clues to guide him. The object couldn't be too big, or the police searchers would have found it by now, and it couldn't be so small that those who had lost it had no hope of finding it again. So, he just kept on the alert for any item concealed from ordinary vision (though not to his) that smacked of the unusual or extraordinary.

He used the metal-detector first. If the object was made of metal, it could not elude his search; if it was not metallic, he had other search modes with which to find it. For example, infrared imaging, in which an inanimate object would appear darker on his screens than the "hotter" organic foliage surrounding it.

Starting from the south border of the grounds, he swept his metal-seeking gaze to the north, deliberately bringing the entire area under his probing beams. The process takes longer to describe than it did to actually conduct the search. Years of constant, intimate familiarity with the hardware had caused Tracker to unconsciously assimilate the processes. He didn't have to think about them, he just did them, just as a reader doesn't stop to think about the mechanical process of scanning lines of type while poring over a page of text.

He had almost reached the limits of his search when he found what he was looking for. The object was in the northwest quadrant of the garden, a sizeable chunk of metal that blazed brightly on his screen. Not only was it obscured by weeds, but it was also in a ditch that doubly concealed it from human eyes. Given time and manpower enough for an exhaustive search, Captain Martel undoubtedly would have turned it up, but Tracker was able to find it sooner, not later.

What had he found? He wasn't sure of that himself. Tagging its location by voice command into his hardware's computer memory, he zoomed in on the image to examine it in greater detail.

At first glance, he almost took it for some kind of gardening tool, a kind of hand-held digger used to rake up the soil. A closer inspection disabused him of that notion. The object looked more like a weapon than a tool. A student (and master) of the martial arts, and a collector of weapons himself, he noticed a strong similarity to such archaic weapons as the Indian *katar*, a punching dagger; and even more closely, to the *Bagh nakh*, the "tiger's claws," also from old India, a kind of knuckle-duster bearing hooked, sickle-shaped metal claws.

The resemblance to the *Bagh nakh* was especially provocative, in that the weapon had been used by brigands to simulate the wounds made by a big cat, and thus mislead the authorities into believing that the victim had been slain by a man-killing beast rather than by cutthroat robbers. Not that Tracker suspected any tie-in between the Caribbean island of Tambour and the subcontinent of India. But the esoteric nature of the weapon might well have cultish significance, and there was much in the mass murders here that also smacked of ritual cult practices.

Despite Captain Martel's downplaying of the extent of voodoo, or vodoun, on the island, Tracker knew from his background briefings that the entire string of islands, from here to Haiti, was the home and center of such practices. Why, even the island's name reflected that fact. Originally discovered and briefly ruled by England, it had been ceded to France during one of the interminable wars of the 18th century. The first French ships that came to take possession of the islands lay offshore for some days, during which their crews were struck by the sound of drumming coming from deep in the interior, where many runaway slaves had fled. Indeed, "Tambour" is the French word for "drum." Over the next two hundred years, many French colonial administrators proudly proclaimed that they had succeeded in suppressing the cult. In the end, the foreign imperialists had been booted out, but apparently the old religion remained.

What connection a cult killing in Tambour had to the death-made-to-look-like-an-accident of aerospace-defense executive Julia Munro was still a mystery to Tracker.

But he had little doubt that he had found what the killers had lost. His immediate problem lay in explaining how he had made the find. He certainly wasn't going to reveal the secrets of his multi-million-dollar hardwired head unless there was no alternative to doing so. Men and women had died (and been killed) to preserve that ultra-classified secret.

Instead, he used the stage magician's classic trick of misdirection. Not revealing his discovery, he ambled around the gardens for ten, fifteen more minutes, making a show of looking under bushes, between tree roots, behind walls, and the like, before he "accidentally" happened to stumble across it and announce his find to the others.

Even with all that, he could see that Captain Martel wasn't buying his cover story. That could turn out to be a problem later. He hoped it wouldn't, since he and the canny police commandant were both on the same side, and Martel was not an antagonist to be underestimated.

For now, though, how the discovery had been made was less important to Martel than the fact of the discovery itself. He knew what the object was, all right, as did his men. Their reactions proved that, especially Bouchard's, whose profound unease communicated a sense of dread about the object. The claw, as Martel had called it.

The claw.

Brought up into the light of day, held suspended in the forks of the rake, there was something about the claw that was disturbing. Menacing. The wickedly hooked prongs had been designed to rip and rake and slash. It was old, old. Tracker knew enough metallurgy to be certain that iron had not been forged and worked in that manner for several hundred years. There were no marks or engravings to be seen on it; if any had existed, they had been worn away long ago.

It was old, but the rawhide thong knotted to the pommel ring was new, and couldn't have been more than a few months old. Tracker could guess its purpose. The rawhide loop allowed the claw to be carried, either secured to a belt or some other item of clothing, or worn slung from the bearer's neck.

And Tracker could guess how it had come to be lost. The thong must have caught on something and come undone as the claw's bearer hoisted himself up the pavilion, preparatory to making the attack. He hadn't noticed it was lost . . . well, he had other things to occupy his mind, like mass murder. He must not have noticed the claw's loss until much later, after the massacre, when it was too late to do anything about it that night. Also, he couldn't have known where it was lost, for the prisoners who were taken the following night had been searching in a different part of the grounds. Tracker had carefully searched that area himself, by wavepulse, and had found nothing.

Finding the claw was a major breakthrough in the case. Tracker knew what Captain Martel meant when he warned of the danger the discovery entailed. Obviously the claw was of major importance to the killers, since some of them had risked capture in a futile attempt to find it. The rest of the gang was still loose, along with an unknown number of confederates.

What would they do to get the claw back?

What *wouldn't* they do?

Danger came sooner than even Tracker suspected, and he knew something that the others didn't: that they were being stalked by at least one unknown assailant.

The first warning had gone unnoticed, even by him. That was when the birds had flown out of a treetop in the north thicket. It registered on his mind, but he had more or less ignored it in the excitement of finding the claw and in the adroit verbal gymnastics he employed to try to disguise his discovery as a lucky accident.

But the second time it happened, he took notice.

Birds were flying into the trees to roost for the night. Birds flying out of the trees went against the grain. When it happened once, it could be written off as just one of those things. As Cressy had suggested, perhaps a cat or some other small predator had stampeded the birds into flight. When it happened again, and closer, Tracker decided to look into it.

He did so in a way that only he could. The keenest human eyes could only see a few inches into any part of the thicket, due to the riotously overgrown foliage.

Tracker's sub-vocal command switched his visor's scope to the infrared imaging mode.

All bodies in the physical universe radiate heat to some extent. The IR imager "saw" heat, which is part of the spectrum invisible to the naked eye. The device was an ingenious by-product of the same technology used in the guidance systems of heat-seeking missiles, sending them homing in on their targets by tracking their heat signature.

The infrared mode showed up on the screen on the inner side of Tracker's lenses. It was a weird, ghostly scene that met his eyes. Plant life, the grass, trees, leaves, flowers, were relatively cool and appeared as feathery, insubstantial veils, semi-transparent. They stood out against the background of inorganic rocks and dirt.

The thicket of trees was hung with countless brightly glowing dots, blazing jewels of light that were birds, with their high metabolic rates.

The manlike figure that crept among the trees of the thicket was a glowing beacon of hot white light.

The hotter a thing was, the brighter it glowed on the IR imager. The skulker's body heat signature registered so strongly on the screen that no amount of foliage could conceal it.

He—Tracker assumed it was a he, though no identifying sexual characteristics could be determined in the blazing human-shaped blob of light—moved low to the ground, twisting and turning to worm his way through the tangled brush. Although the thicket looked impenetrable from the outside, there were numerous game trails and passages honeycombing it.

The skulker cradled a long straight dark object against his body. Its shadowy form tagged it as an inanimate object, while its shape and the way it was held indicated that it was a weapon of some sort.

The overgrown woods both helped and hampered the stalker. They hid him from view but hindered his movements. He might have climbed a tree to better see what the gendarmes were up to, and thus caused the birds to scatter in panic, or perhaps a clumsy misstep had disturbed the birds into fleeing. Either way, he was definitely working his way toward the investigators. His stealth and the weapon showed that he was up to no good.

Tracker had a problem. How could he warn the others of the gunman's approach without further displaying his astonishing abilities?

The gunman wouldn't shoot, not yet. There were still too many trees between him and the gendarmes for him to even see them, much less get a clear shot at them. He would either have to climb another tree for a sniper's perch or make his way to the edge of the thicket.

Judging from the direction in which he was moving, he was angling across the thicket toward a point at its edge that would put him directly in line with his human targets.

Tension mounted in Tracker as he monitored the stalker's steady progress toward his goal. He would have to warn the others, and soon, even at the risk of betraying his powers.

Suddenly, gunfire.

The shooting took Tracker as much by surprise as it did the others, since he had been concentrating on the gunman in the woods. The skulker, though close, was still too far away from the open to risk a shot.

But the shot hadn't come from the woods; it had come from the front of the house. A cry of pain was cut short by a second shot.

Captain Martel and his men were stung into action after a brief pause to make some sense out of what had happened. Bouchard was the first to respond with the others close behind his heels.

Whatever had happened, it was a godsend to Tracker, providing him with the distraction he needed. Martel shouted to him to follow, and so Tracker did. He followed the gendarmes into the house, but not far. While the others thundered down the long hall toward the front of the house,

Tracker ducked into the narrow passageway to the right, the one leading into the kitchen.

A high narrow window with a pointed arch opened in the wall, letting light into the hallway. Crouching low beside it, Tracker peeked through the corner at the pavilion and gardens.

No more than a few heartbeats later, he saw a figure burst out of the woods and run up the garden path toward the north side of the château. The gunman was sinewy, athletic, in his late twenties. He wore a camouflaged fatigue shirt, open and unbuttoned to show an olive drab T-shirt beneath it; a web belt, camo fatigue pants, combat boots. He toted a submachine gun with a folding metal frame stock and a cone-shaped silencer that was almost as long as the weapon itself. His face was a tiger-striped devil mask.

He flashed past Tracker's view, moving beyond his sightline. Tracker bitterly regretted not being armed, but that was a sacrifice he had had to make in the interest of decent working relations with his Tambourian hosts. A nicety of protocol that now might doom them all.

Solid walls now stood between Tracker and the gunman, but that didn't stop the American from monitoring the other's progress. Tracker could have looked through the soild wall with his IR imager, but the picture would have been cloudily vague at best. But there was another, better way.

He activated the miniaturized directional microphones built into his computerized visor. They were filament-shaped rods placed inside the long axes of the visor's earpieces, linked into the sub-cranial bone-phone implant behind his right ear.

The auditory implant was a two-way comm link. Just as it picked up his unvoiced commands and transmitted them to the visor's computerized control center, they also functioned in reverse.

That is, they could receive the sounds picked up by his directional mini-microphones and relay them to Tracker by vibrating through the bone of his skull into the hearing apparatus of his right-side inner ear. It was an unpleasant sensation to hear things that way, something like a maddening itch inside his ear, but it worked and had saved his life on more than one occasion. Unpleasant or not, it was better than being dead.

It worked now. Clomping sounds, loud as an elephant's tread, boomed inside his ear, making him wince with pain. He subvocally commanded the pick-up to modulate the volume. The footsteps were still loud, though not painful for him to hear.

He was hearing the sounds of the gunman moving outside through the walls. And not just his heavy-footed tread. Tracker could hear the other's harsh panting breath rasping in his lungs, the rattle of equipment on his web belt, the rustle of fabric as the clothes moved on his body, even the beating of his heart. It was beating very fast, pounding away like a trip hammer, reflecting the extreme emotional state of a man who is poised to kill.

There was something almost obscenely intimate about such auditory communion, but Tracker couldn't afford scruples about that. The other was a killer zeroing in on a mission of death.

And coming closer. The footsteps slowed as he rounded the southwest corner of the house, drawing abreast of Tracker.

Tracker swung into action, gliding sideways down the hallway into the kitchen. His movements were suggestive of those used by basketball players moving sideways down the court, but were actually quite different in origin.

Tracker was in the side stance of Tae Kwon Do, the Korean martial art at which he was adept. The style emphasized deep fighting stances, powerful kicks, and lethal hand techniques. Tracker was in the famous horse stance, with feet spread wide apart and legs bent.

Moving sideways, he flashed down the hallway as quietly as a shadow, then into the kitchen.

Outside, the gunman hesitated, slowing. Tracker could guess what was going on in his mind. Originally planning to circle around to the front of the house to ambush his targets, he now caught sight of the side door into the kitchen and decided to change his plans. He would enter the house, go through it, and take his prey from behind.

The kitchen had a tile floor, long countertops, cabinets, a stove, refrigerator, microwave oven, and all the latest modern conveniences. It seemed doubly spic and span since it was one of the few areas in the murder house not stained with blood.

In the middle of the floor stood a wooden butcher's block table. Suspended overhead from the ceiling was a four-sided metal rack whose hooks and pegs were hung with a variety of cooking utensils. There were pots and pans of every size and shape, whisks, collanders, strainers, sifters, grinders. A wide selection of stainless steel cutlery was in a wooden holder on the table.

The gunman had made his decision and no longer hesitated. He moved toward the house, nearing the side door. Tracker grabbed the biggest knife in the holder and went to meet him.

The door was hinged on the left so it would open in that direction. Tracker padded to it and flattened his back against the wall on the right side. He switched off the directional microphones. They weren't needed now; he could hear the gunman's approach with his normal hearing.

The gunman was cautious enough to try the door first, rattling the knob. It didn't turn. It was locked. The gunman stepped back, took a deep breath, then kicked the door wide open. It swung back on its hinges, slamming into the wall hard enough to crack the plaster. The gunman came rushing through the doorway into the kitchen.

Glimpsing Tracker out of the corner of his eye, he moved, but not fast enough. Tracker's left palm slapped down onto the top of the gun barrel, locking onto it with a viselike grip. He pulled forward on it, yanking the gunman in the direction he was already going.

Crying out, the gunman lurched forward, off-balance. He tried to swing the gun around but could make no headway against Tracker's grip. His feet skittered on the tiled floor.

For an instant, the two antagonists were so close that each could feel the other's breath on his face.

The gunman's face was elaborately painted in a greasy gray and green tiger-stripe pattern. More than camouflage, it was a mask. His eyes widened, showing all whites around the irises.

Now that the gunman was off-balance, Tracker crashed into him from the side, slamming him against the pantry door so hard that it rocked on its hinges. Then he buried the butcher knife in the gunman's chest, in the soft part of the belly just below the breastbone. It went in easily enough, through him and out his back, pinning him to the pantry door.

The gunman tried to scream but couldn't, since a strike in that important nerve center has a paralyzing effect. The blow had been delivered with such force that it lifted the gunman off his feet, pinning him to the door with his soles dangling a few inches above the floor. Mortally wounded, his face contorted in a silent shriek.

Tracker gave the blade a vicious corkscrewing twist to the right, severing the spinal column and delivering instant death. The dead man slumped, a puppet with its strings cut. His open eyes were already starting to glaze over.

Tracker let go of the knife handle. The corpse stayed in place, still pinned to the pantry door. Tracker plucked the submachine gun from the other's lifeless grip. Good thing the safety was still on, or the gunman's convulsive death grip might have triggered a burst.

"You don't mind if I borrow this? Thanks so much," Tracker said, muttering.

The weapon was the finest of its kind, top-quality hardware made in the USA. There might be an angle in that, but Tracker doubted it. The government had sold thousands of this model to friendly governments throughout the hemisphere, many of which were then resold to less legitimate parties, such as death squads and drug dealers, so there were a lot of them in circulation.

Not that Tracker was knocking the arms sales. He was just damn glad that Uncle Sammy was still making a product that foreigners wanted to buy. Had to reverse that negative balance of payments somehow. But it didn't bode too well for tracing the chain of ownership.

What else did the corpse have to offer in the way of clues? A green canvas bag was clipped to the side of his web belt. Inside, it was filled with spare clips of ammunition. "You came loaded for bear, eh? Thanks, I can use these, too." Tracker grabbed a few handfuls of clips and stuffed them into various pockets of his safari jacket.

A quick search of the dead man was all Tracker could handle, not because he was unnerved by the corpse he had so recently made, but because he wanted to rejoin Captain Martel and the others as soon as possible. He had a feeling that the action was far from over.

The buttoned-down breast pocket of the fatigue shirt yielded an unusual find: a glass vial about the size and shape of a man's pinky, sealed with a rubber stopper and filled with a dark, murky, viscous liquid whose foul smell leaked out despite the seal. If it was a drug of some kind, it was unlike any in Tracker's experience. He found a dishrag near the sink, wrapped the vial in its folds, and pocketed it.

A survival knife the size of a small sword hung in a sheath strapped to the dead man's side, opposite the ammo pouch. There was nothing in it for Tracker so he left it there. "My knife is better," Tracker said.

A quick pat-down of the other's pockets unearthed nothing of interest. Significantly, the gunman carried no wallet, no papers, no identification of any kind. The hallmark of a professional killer.

But there was something interesting to be found on the other's face and left ear. Tracker had missed the detail at first, because it was hidden under the greasy tiger-striped makeup. The dead man's cheek on the right side of his face was marked with a series of three diagonal scars, incised one above the other. The marks were similar to the ritual scarification sported by warlike tribesmen in various rugged locales around the globe.

The lobe of his left ear was similarly marked with three parallel slashes. They were small, barely a quarter-inch wide each, but quite distinctive.

A thin tarnished chain hung around his neck. Tracker took hold of it and fished out the object attached to it. "Ahhhh . . . paydirt," he breathed.

Dangling from the other end of the chain was a small amulet, or charm, a little larger than a silver dollar. It was a replica in miniature of the claw that Tracker had found earlier in the weeds below the pavilion wall. "It's all starting to make sense now," he said.

Taking hold of the chain, he tore it off the corpse's neck with such violence that it marked the flesh. He dropped it into an inside breast pocket and buttoned the flap tightly.

6.

"WHERE IS TRACKER?"

That was the question puzzling Captain Martel and his two gendarmes, Corporal Bouchard and Constable Cressy. Groux was dead and Octave, his murderer, had absconded with the car. For the moment, there was nothing to be done about either matter.

The American's disappearance was another matter, one especially vexing to Martel, since it piled mystery on mystery and added additional complications at the worst possible time.

"I never trusted that one from the start," Bouchard said. "The way he found the claw when no one else could was positively uncanny! It would not surprise me if he was part of it, in on the whole business right from the start!"

"If that is so, then why did he turn the claw over to us, instead of waiting until later to tell his confederates of its location? Then none of us would have been the wiser," Martel said.

"That shows what a deep game he's playing," Bouchard said stubbornly.

"And how could he have known where it was?"

"The killer must have told him where it was," Bouchard began, then faltered. "But no, if they knew where it was, then they would have gotten it themselves on the night after the murders, so that doesn't make sense either," he said, stroking his chin.

"In any case, M. Tracker is a man who bears watching. Which we can't do because we have lost sight of him!" Martel said.

"Perhaps he is hiding somewhere, afraid for his life because of the shooting," Bouchard suggested.

"Perhaps, but he struck me as a cool customer, and one who is not easily alarmed. Still, who knows how a man will react under fire? Your suggestion may well have merit, Bouchard."

Captain Martel and Bouchard stood in the drive, facing the front of the house. Jack Lashbrook sat slumped in the chair, shaking, facing them, while Cressy stood a few feet away.

"Is he in the house, Cressy?" Martel said.

"I will see, Captain."

Cressy turned, went to the doorway, and peered inside. The long hall was empty of all but the lengthening shadows of oncoming night. Cressy started to step inside, across the threshold, when an instinctive sense of caution made him draw his gun. With Groux dead, Octave gone, and Tracker missing, who knew what dangers threatened?

He went a few paces deeper into the house, the vast front hall seeming to magnify his soft footfalls. He called Tracker's name a few times to no response. Before venturing deeper, he heard Martel calling him. Retracing his steps, he returned to the threshold and stood framed in the doorway, filling it with his large form.

"Well?" Martel said.

"If he's inside, he's not answering my calls," Cressy said. "Do you want me to search for him, Captain?"

"No," Martel said, "it's best that we not divide our forces now. We've already lost a man, and that's one man too many."

"You think the American had something to do with Groux's death, Captain?" Bouchard asked.

"I don't see how. He was with us when Groux was shot. Besides, he's never set foot on this island before yesterday; I know that for a fact. Still, this is a most murky affair where nothing is as it seems, so no possibility can be ruled out. After all, who would have expected Octave to turn out to be one of *them* instead of one of us?"

"Certainly not Groux," Cressy said.

"No, not Groux. His death proves his innocence," Martel said.

Bouchard said, "But how could Octave be one of *them*? He doesn't bear any of the marks of the society."

"Would he have been allowed to join the police if he had?" Martel asked.

"No, certainly not! Ah, I take your meaning," Bouchard said. "They plan well ahead, those cunning devils!"

"If they could plant one of their number among us, they could plant more than one," Cressy said.

"We can take some comfort in knowing that none of us three is also a traitor, since each of us has had the chance to shoot the others in the back but none of us has taken it," Martel said.

"Well, what now, Captain?" Cressy said.

"We may expect danger, deadly danger, to strike at us any moment now, and from the most unexpected quarter," Martel said.

Jack Lashbrook had been sitting slumped forward on the bench, holding his face in his hands and moaning softly. On hearing Martel's last remarks, he sat up and took notice. "I don't understand, Captain Martel," he said. "I mean, I don't understand any of it, the senseless killing, but mainly I don't get what you're talking about when you say that we're in some kind of danger. I mean, it's awful about Groux— horrible!—but why should that threaten the rest of us?"

"Octave did not kill Groux and steal the car merely to discomfort us, monsieur. He did it for a reason, and that was to abandon us to the tender mercies of his murderous brethren, with whom he is no doubt already in contact," Martel said.

"Who—? Not the people who committed the massacre?"

"Yes, monsieur, and others of the same fraternity."

"They wouldn't try to kill us!" Lashbrook said, choking.

Martel could almost smile at the other's naiveté. Almost. "That is what I have been trying to tell you," he said.

"My God!" Lashbrook jumped to his feet. He said, "We've got to get out of here!"

"And so we shall," Martel assured him.

"My nerves are shot," Lashbrook said, quavering. "I can't take much more of this—"

"Losing your head will only worsen our predicament, monsieur. I can assure you that my men and I will protect you to the best of our ability, even with our lives, if necessary," Martel said.

"What good is that to me if I get killed, too? My God!"

"It would be of slight consolation to us, too, M. Lashbrook. At any rate, we must prepare ourselves to make the best of a bad situation."

"My God!"

But Lashbrook wasn't bewailing his fate this time. He was crying aloud at the act of violence taking place right that second before his horrified eyes.

A whispering stutter sounded: *Pht-pht-pht-pht-pht-pht!*

Virtually simultaneously with the sound, a section of trees and bushes opposite the southeast corner of the house, on the far side of the driveway, was ripped and torn by an invisible hail. Leaves were shredded into green confetti, tree branches were truncated, stems and branches exploded into clouds of pulp and sap.

The whispered stutter ceased.

The invisible hail stopped, too.

A bulky figure rose at the edge of the south thicket where the hail had fallen. It crouched, cradling something in its arms.

Pht-pht-pht-pht-pht!

A fresh burst of hail peppered the figure. It fell over sideways, away from where the lethal burst was coming. It bounced off a tree, fell forward, and came crashing to earth face-down at the edge of the thicket.

It had all happened so fast that the gendarmes barely had time to blink before the would-be killer hit the ground, dead.

"My God," Lashbrook said. He gulped, swallowing hard.

A voice rang out from around the corner of the house: "Don't shoot! It's me, Tracker! I'm coming out!"

A few seconds later, Tracker came walking into view. Thin wisps of smoke curled from the mouth of the suppressor on the silenced submachine gun, which he toted barrel down.

"Ah, M. Tracker . . . I was just about to give you up for lost," Captain Martel said.

"I felt the same way about you," Tracker said, "especially when I spotted that shooter in the bushes taking a bead on you. Lucky thing I got to him first."

"You are a man to whom Fortune seems to have taken a liking."

"If I was really lucky, I'd be back home right now, having a brew and watching a football game on TV."

"But you are in my home now, monsieur. And may I ask you if you would be so good as to put down your weapon?"

"It's down. Anyway, it's not pointing at you," Tracker said.

"I would feel better if you turned it over to me."

"But I'd feel worse. This is a mighty unfriendly little island you've got, Captain. A man without a gun on Tambour is a man undressed."

Bouchard and Cressy raised their guns to cover Tracker. "Do as the Captain says and throw down your weapon," Bouchard said.

"Like hell! Wise up, men. If I wanted you dead all I had to do was let that joker in the bushes pull the trigger on you. You've got your hands full without picking a fight with me. Anyway, I don't intend to be the only guy without a gun around here. One of your cops already turned traitor. How do I know that there's not another one like him?" Tracker said.

"Let it go," Martel told his men. "What he says is true. If he meant to do us harm, he had ample opportunity to do so. Besides, we're going to need all the fighting men we can get."

Bouchard and Cressy pointed their guns elsewhere than at Tracker, but they didn't put them away. Things were happening too fast to indulge in the luxury of a holstered gun.

"Bah! I don't trust him," Bouchard said.

"I'll worry about that. You go and check the dead man," Martel said.

"Yes, Captain."

Bouchard trotted over to the corpse.

"Careful," Tracker said, "there might be a few more of them hiding in the bushes."

Bouchard glared at him, then thought about what he had said. He peered into the brush, nosing around, parting branches with the tip of his gun. Rising on tiptoes, he craned to see deeper into the dark thicket, which was growing steadily darker and more obscure as the last light of day faded from the sky.

"Where did you get the gun, M. Tracker?" Martel asked.

"I stole it fair and square. There was another one like him," Tracker said, indicating the dead man.

"What happened to him?"

"I saw him trying to sneak in through the side door, so I hid and waited for him. He had a close encounter with a piece of kitchen cutlery. Most regrettable."

"Not really."

"No, not really, Captain."

Tracker reached into his breast pocket and fished out the claw-shaped amulet. "He was wearing this."

"Ah!"

Bouchard, down on one knee beside the body of the second shooter, pulled back the dead man's collar, saw a chain, took hold of it, and tore it loose. It, too, bore a claw amulet. Clutching the chain by the ends, Bouchard held the amulet aloft, noticeably careful to keep it away from his body, as if he feared being contaminated by the touch of the claw. "Look! He has one, too," he said.

"And that's not all. I found something else, Captain. Tell me if this means anything to you," Tracker said. Taking out the folded dishrag square from his pocket, he placed it in Martel's outstretched palm. "It's wrapped up, a little glass bottle with some nasty-looking shit inside."

Martel unfolded the wrapping, baring the bottle. His narrowed eyes gleamed as he gripped the vial between thumb and forefinger and held it against the fast-fading light. He sniffed it, his nostrils crinkling in delicate disgust when he got a good whiff of the odor.

"The *borfima*, Captain," said Cressy, who had come up beside Martel.

"Yes, the *borfima*," Martel agreed.

"What's a *borfima*?" Tracker asked.

"A vile potion, compounded of drugs, herbs, roots, and essences of various vital organs, taken by the *Egbo* executioners to increase their power," Martel said. "Bouchard, see if the other one has the *borfima* as well," he told the corporal.

Bouchard rolled the dead man on his back. The corpse was outfitted similarly to the assassin whom Tracker had killed, in camouflaged fatigues and combat boots. His face was painted the same way, with tiger-striped swirls of greasy green and gray streaking his face into a ferocious mask. His eyes were open and staring. He was short, squat, powerfully built, with wide sloping shoulders and a thick torso. Slugs from the silenced submachine gun which Tracker had turned on him had torn out most of his middle. Strands of a brownish-green mucous-like substance were smeared in the corners of his lips.

"He must have already taken the potion, Captain," Bouchard announced. "There's traces of it on his mouth."

"Do you recognize him?" Martel asked.

"I don't think so, Captain. It's hard to tell, because of the face paint, but he doesn't look like anyone I've ever seen before," Bouchard said.

"I'm not surprised. They're bringing in outsiders to do their dirty work. They don't have enough *Bati Yeli* of their own on the island, apparently . . . for which the saints be praised," Martel said. "*Bati Yeli* . . . that means 'executioners,' M. Tracker," he added.

"I had a hunch it meant something like that," Tracker said. "Those two are part of what you called *Egbo*?"

"Yes. They are *Egbo* . . . or at least they were."

"Octave couldn't have summoned them in this short of a time," Cressy said.

"No," Martel said, "these two must have been here all

along, hiding in the bush, keeping an eye on things, serving as watchdogs for their masters. Most probably Octave was unaware of their presence, or he wouldn't have taken such drastic measures to pass the word that the claw had been found. Instead of fleeing, he might have tried to kill all of us if he had known that the others were nearby to assist him. Finding the claw has dealt the cult a serious setback, provided that we live long enough to deliver it where it can do the most good.

"There may be others lurking nearby," he added, "so stay alert, all of you."

Bouchard took possession of the submachine gun and the full ammo pouch that had belonged to the second shooter. "A fine weapon," he said, running his fingers over the gun. "Better than anything we have in the police arsenal!"

"Yes," Martel said, "they are well-armed and well-financed, to be sure. Hold onto that, Bouchard, you may be able to put it to good use in the very near future."

"Yes, *mon capitaine*."

Bouchard fixed the ammo pouch to the side of his gunbelt, over his left hip. He held the weapon across his chest, with one hand on the barrel just behind the silencer and the other hand on the stock. He seemed ready, vigilant, and eager to use it.

"Now we've both got machine guns," Tracker said to him.

"Bah," Bouchard said.

"Well, what now, Captain?" Tracker asked.

"We can't stay here. Others will be coming soon," Martel said.

"More *Bati Yeli*?"

"Yes, monsieur, more *Bati Yeli*."

"Why don't we set a trap for them, Captain? We could make things pretty hot for them."

"I like your spirit, but I fear that would not be practical. We have only two machine guns and a few handguns between us. They will come in force and be heavily armed.

"No, our best hope is to get back to town, to police headquarters. I cannot explain it to you now, but our best hope of smashing this vile cult—and, incidentally, saving our own lives—is to deliver the claw to certain persons who will know what to do with it," Martel said.

"It's your party," Tracker said. "Any chance of calling for reinforcements?"

"Unfortunately, the phone lines are down on Fire Ridge. They were sabotaged on the night of the murders, presumably by the killers, to prevent anyone from calling for help or reporting any suspicious behavior in the neighborhood. Things move slowly here on our little island, and the damage has not yet been repaired. Otherwise, I would suggest that we avail ourselves of one of the neighbors' phones for just that purpose, but the entire ridge is cut off from communication. And of course, I cannot radio in to headquarters for assistance, since the radio is in the car which was stolen by Octave."

"Maybe we could borrow a car from one of the neighbors."

"The people of Tambour expect the police to protect them, monsieur. They do not expect to protect the police, especially not the rich tax-paying citizens of Fire Ridge. But there is another, more serious consideration. You have observed the murderousness of our opponents. I cannot in good conscience involve civilians in this affair, especially not when they might become targets for helping us. I will not see the horrors which happened here repeated on other poor unfortunates."

"If you say so, Captain."

"Yes, M. Tracker, I say so."

"What do we do then? Start walking?"

"Hopefully that will not be necessary. There are a number of vehicles in the garage on this property. We will commandeer one of them and take it back to town," Martel said.

"Sounds good to me. I'm ready when you are."

"We will go now," Martel said. "You strike me as a fighting man, M. Tracker."

"Oh, I've been in a few scrapes in my time," Tracker said off-handedly.

"Well, you're in one now," Martel said.

The police captain eyed Jack Lashbrook to see how he

was holding up under the strain. The young consular assistant was obviously in over his depth. He exhibited some of the symptoms of a man in a state of shock. He was pale, deathly pale. He stared off into the distance, nervously gnawing on a knuckle with his fine even white teeth. His body posture was stiff, angular, strained.

Lowering his voice so that Lashbrook could not hear him, Captain Martel confided, "Frankly, M. Tracker, we face formidable obstacles. The odds against us are not good."

"That's okay, Captain. I like to play the longshots myself," Tracker said.

Martel nodded. He addressed his next remarks to the whole group. "Attention, please! We will proceed to the garage now, so everyone stay together and remain alert," he said.

The men formed up. Bouchard was armed with the submachine gun, so he took the point. Captain Martel and Constable Cressy took the flanks, Jack Lashbrook was in the middle, and Tracker, armed with the other submachine gun, brought up the rear.

The garage was a two-door outbuilding located off to the side of the northeast corner of the château. The group made a beeline for it, crossing open ground. Jack Lashbrook, however, stumbled along like an automaton, mechanically lifting one foot and putting it down in front of the other.

"How're you making it, Jack?" Tracker asked.

"My God," Lashbrook said, groaning.

Tracker punched him playfully on the shoulder. "Cheer up," he said, "and look on the bright side. If you live through this, you're sure to get a promotion!"

7.

THERE WERE TWO cars in the garage, a rugged gold-colored Chevy station wagon and a spiffy little late-model Peugeot sedan. Both cars were gassed up and appeared to be in good working order. But the keys were nowhere to be found.

"Let's take the wagon," Tracker said. "It's bigger and it's got a lot more muscle. We might need it to power out of a tight spot."

"You have overlooked one small detail, monsieur. How are we going to start the car without the keys?" Martel asked.

"Perhaps he will find the keys the same way that he found the claw," Bouchard suggested.

"My so-called 'evil eyes' don't seem so bad when they're working in your favor, eh, Corporal?" Tracker said.

"I do not care to joke about the subject," Bouchard said.

"Well, I hate to disappoint you, but I haven't got the slightest idea of where they are," Tracker said. That was true. Tracker had swept the garage with his metal-detecting beams, to no avail. Wherever the keys were, they weren't in the garage.

"They might be in the house. I will see," offered Cressy.

"Don't bother. I'll have the car started up in a jiffy," Tracker said.

A pair of pliers would have helped, but there weren't any

in the garage. There was a tire iron on top of a wooden bench on one side of the garage, and that would suit Tracker's purpose.

The station wagon was unlocked, so Tracker didn't have to break a window to get in. The obvious places for stashing a set of keys had already been searched: tucked up inside the sun visor, in the ash tray, under the dashboard, below the rubber floor mats, and under the seats. The keys weren't in any of those places.

Climbing behind the steering wheel, Tracker held the tire iron in both hands, leading with the thin chisel-shaped point. He slammed it into the place where the locked ignition was set into the steering column. Nothing happened the first time, so he gave it a few more good hard shots in the same place.

Part of the locking device was wedged free of the column. Tracker wedged the tip of the tire iron into the space and worked it back and forth, trying to pry it off. One good maximum effort managed to do it. The locking device popped free from the column, trailing a number of wires. Tracker tore the wires free of the locking assembly and threw it away. Stripping the insulation off the ends of the wires, baring them, he touched them together in various combinations. Sparks zapped on the ends of the wires. While he was working them, he played with the gas pedal, giving it some gas.

The engine coughed and jerked with a few fitful starts and misfires. Contact was made, and the motor suddenly roared to life, belching exhaust clouds from the tail pipe.

Bouchard stood outside the open garage doors, armed with the submachine gun, keeping watch for stealthy attackers. When the car was switched on, he said, "He's not only a witch, he's a car thief, too!"

"You like walking better?" Tracker said.

Captain Martel leaned over the driver's side window. "Bravo, monsieur! Although generally I prefer to lock up those who possess such talents as you have just displayed."

"All in a good cause, Captain. Besides, a good hunter knows the habits of his prey."

"And what kind of hunter are you? A manhunter?"

"I'm just an ordinary American citizen on an unofficial fact-finding mission, Captain."

"It's wonderful, the way you can tell such lies with a straight face. No, don't bother to deny it. I know how you cloak-and-dagger types are in love with your cover stories—" Captain Martel broke off in a fit of coughing, unable to speak due to the clouds of exhaust filling the confined space. He hurried outside to join the others.

Tracker put the car in gear and eased it out of the garage. He put it in park and got out from behind the wheel. "You men know the terrain, not me, so one of you better drive," he said.

"This is Constable Cressy's district, so he knows these mountain roads better than any of us," Martel said. "You drive, Cressy."

"Yes, sir," Cressy said.

Before getting in the car, Cressy turned his gun belt around, so that his holstered gun was on his left hip butt-outward. Wearing his gun this way would allow for a quicker draw from a sitting position. He climbed into the driver's seat. He was a big man, but the seat didn't require any adjustment. It was already set back as far as it could go to make room for Tracker while he was hot-wiring the ignition.

"It'll run okay as long as the motor doesn't stop," Tracker said. "If it does, it'll have to be restarted the same way."

Cressy nodded.

"Why don't I ride up front in the passenger's seat?" Tracker suggested to Martel. "I've got pretty good eyes and can see trouble coming from a long way off."

"No doubt about that! But won't wearing those sunglasses affect your vision now that night is coming?" Martel asked.

"Not at all. Like I said, my eyes are light-sensitive. Not just sunlight. I need the protection at night, too, but they won't hamper my vision. You've already had proof of that."

"Indeed. A most curious eye ailment, however . . ."

"It's nothing serious. I just spent too much time under a sunlamp. Doctor says it should go away in a few months."

"Your eyes haven't failed us so far, so I'll just have to take your word that they will continue to function."

"You can count on it, Captain."

"Very well, monsieur."

"Besides, Bouchard should be relieved that I'm not sitting behind him with a gun. I don't think he trusts me," Tracker added.

"You may be sure of that," Bouchard said.

"Since you've already gotten involved in this matter, we might as well observe the formalities and make it legal," Martel said. "I hereby deputize you as one of my special assistants, M. Tracker."

"Well, thanks. I appreciate the honor," Tracker said.

"Your appointment is temporary and will last for the duration of the current state of emergency. I will also make it retroactive to prevent any legal difficulties arising from your killing the two assassins."

"Terrific. Are you going to swear me in or anything?"

"That will not be necessary," Martel said. "And now let us be on our way."

Tracker got in the passenger side of the front seat, holding the submachine gun upright with the muzzle sticking out of the open window. Martel and Jack Lashbrook got in the back seat.

Bouchard sat in the rear cargo area. He could shoot out of the back window at any pursuers or perch on top of the tailgate and fire forward across the roof at any oncoming attackers.

Cressy put the car in gear. The station wagon rolled down a gravel path for a dozen yards or so before merging with the main driveway.

Martel told Cressy to stop the car as it drew abreast of Groux's dead body. "I will not leave him behind," Martel said. "If I do, the cult might mutilate and desecrate his remains for some of their obscene rituals."

The tailgate was lowered and the cargo hatch opened, revealing a sizable well. A spare tire nestled in the bottom of the space, but there was still plenty of room. Martel and Bouchard took hold of the body by the arms and legs, lugged it to the back of the car, and loaded it as gently as circumstances would allow into the well. Groux lay in a fetal position, curled up on top of the spare tire. The hatch was lowered, Bouchard climbed into the back, the tailgate was raised, and Martel got into the car.

Cressy eased the car forward, down the driveway. The front door of the château gaped wide open, a dark toothless mouth waiting to swallow up the unwary.

That phase of twilight had arrived in which every detail stands out with crystal clarity against its surroundings. The ornate pink château, with its turrets, gables, buttresses, and leaded glass windows, looked like an enchanted palace in an illustration from a book of fairy tales. Or, more accurately, a haunted palace.

"Truly, a house of death," Martel said.

The car picked up speed as it rolled down the long curving driveway toward the main gate. Tracker stuck his head out the window and looked. The others did likewise, but unlike them, Tracker really *looked*. The car slowed to make the turn as they neared the main gate.

"Hit the brakes and come to a full stop about twenty feet in front of the gate," Tracker told Cressy.

Captain Martel saw Cressy glancing in the rearview mirror at him, looking for his reaction. "Do as he says, Cressy. He's been right so far," Martel said.

"Yes, Captain," Cressy said.

"Don't brake too hard or you might stall the motor," Tracker said, "but make sure you come to a complete stop and hold it there until I tell you to go on."

"All right," Cressy said.

"What new trick is this?" Bouchard demanded from the back seat.

"It's a surprise," Tracker said.

Tension mounted as the car neared the main gate. The ridge road was empty, and there was no one in sight.

"Ready," Tracker said. "A little more, a little more—*stop!*"

Cressy stepped on the brake. The car nosed downward. It was going slowly at the time so it stopped easily enough.

A stuttered coughing sound broke from the decorative bushes on the right side of the drive near the open gate. Bullets ripped through empty air where the car would have been if it had kept on going at its original rate of speed. The snout of Tracker's machine gun was poking out over the top of the door as he squeezed off a series of quick sharp bursts.

Slugs tore into the clump of bushes from which the original shots had come. They impacted into an unseen solid body with a sound like a mallet pounding a side of beef. The sound of the hits was louder than the shots from the silenced machine gun.

The car's right front door sliced open. Tracker swung his legs out of the car, put his feet on the tarmac, hopped up, and double-timed toward the bushes.

Parting the branches, he vanished into the foliage for a moment. When he popped back into view, he triumphantly bore aloft not one but *two* machine guns: his own and the one he had taken from the dead assassin who lay stretched out on the ground behind the bushes, riddled with bullets from Tracker's gun. Tracker passed the newly acquired weapon through the right side window to Martel, who eagerly reached for it. "This goes with it," he said, handing the police captain a full ammo pouch that he had also taken from the corpse.

He stuck a fist in front of Martel's face and opened it palm-up. Nestled in his palm was another claw-and-chain amulet. "You can start up a collection of these," he said.

Martel took the sinister charm and pocketed it.

Tracker had used up a fair amount of ammo gunning down the assassin in front of the house and now the one at the gate. He shucked the nearly empty clip out of the receiver, cast it aside, fed in a fresh clip. He slapped the bottom of the clip with his palm heel to make sure it was securely lodged. He locked and loaded the weapon and was ready to rumble again.

He hopped back into the front seat, closed the door.

Cressy glanced at him. "Is it safe to go now, monsieur?" he asked.

"I don't know how safe it is, but there aren't any more

killers on the immediate horizon, as far as I can tell," Tracker said.

"That's good enough for me," Cressy said.

He cornered around the stone pillar and turned right on the ridge road. The car headed south on the two-lane blacktop that ran parallel to Fire Ridge. Bouchard grumbled in the back, darkly muttering about the evil eye and other sorcerous matters.

"I could almost agree with the corporal that you are a witch, M. Tracker. How you knew there was an assassin at the gate is beyond me," Martel said.

"I'll let you in on a little secret, Captain," Tracker said.

"Please do."

"I'm part–Sioux Indian. We've got a sixth sense about such things."

"That's as good an explanation as any I've gotten from you."

"Actually, I played a hunch. Your cult killers seem to do things by threes. There were three hooks on the claw. Three killers went inside the house on the night of the massacre, and three stayed outside. Three came back the following night, when you caught two and the other one got away. Since they like to do things in threes, I figured that there'd be three members of this hit team. I got two, so there had to be a third hanging around someplace. The gate looked like a good place for an ambush, since the car would have to come to almost a complete stop to make the turn. So I was keeping my eyes peeled in that direction, and when I saw something moving around in the bushes, I was pretty sure that it was Killer Number Three. I had Cressy hit the brakes before we reached there, and that startled the assassin into shooting ahead of schedule. I saw where the shooting was coming from and poured a mess of lead in there. And that's all there was to it," Tracker said.

That wasn't all there was to it, of course. Tracker's line of reasoning as explained to Martel was more or less truthful, as far as it went. He had noticed the recurrence of the number three in the rituals and actions of the cult, and felt sure that there was a third killer lying somewhere in wait on the grounds.

As the car rolled down the drive, he had scanned the route with the infrared imager of his screen scope. Once again, the body heat of the hidden attacker had made him stand out like a neon sign to the meta-vision of Tracker. Knowing the ambusher lay in wait, Tracker had set an ambush of his own. The brush that hid the killer from normal eyes was clear as glass to Tracker, who was able to draw as clear a bead on the killer as if he were standing out in the open.

But of such matters he said nothing.

The police captain sighed with resignation, knowing somehow that there was more to the explanation than Tracker had told him, much more, but that the rest of the story would not soon be forthcoming. Besides, not knowing of Tracker's high-tech hyper-senses, the American's facile explanations were as logical as any Martel could imagine. The only other alternative was to plunge into the realm of the supernatural à la Bouchard, and ascribe Tracker's amazing abilities to the powers of witchery and magic. That was a line of thought that Martel would prefer not to pursue. The entire affair was already steeped in the darkest currents of ritual murder and ancient evil.

"So, shall we say that you had another 'lucky guess,' monsieur?" Martel said.

"That's as good a way to describe it as any," Tracker said. "And now let me ask you a question, Captain."

"Yes?"

"You were interrupted a few times, so you never did quite get around to telling me what *Egbo* is."

"It is an ancient and murderous secret society, monsieur," Captain Martel said. "*Egbo* is the cult of the Leopard Men!"

8.

Tracker had heard of the Leopard Men.

He had never heard the word *Egbo*, which means "Leopard Society," in the language indigenous to a broad belt of tribal peoples on the west coast of Africa, particularly the area now comprising Nigeria and Sierra Leone.

But he had heard of the Leopard Men. The tale had been told to him about ten years earlier, during a sensitive mission in Central America when the Sandinista-Contra clash was hot.

It had been a one-shot deal. Tracker had gone into the mountains on the border to oversee the installation of a network of aircraft detection devices along critical air corridors.

His host on the mission had been a band of mercenaries working as "advisors" to the rebels. The mercs had been recruited through a supposedly neutral third party to avoid the fingerprints of U.S. government involvement, which was forbidden by an act of Congress. Tracker worked a similar ploy to cover his participation in the deal. He spent a few miserable weeks in the mountains, installing the self-powered radar pods on inaccessible ledges and peaks and working the bugs out of the system so it wouldn't mistake a friendly for an enemy aircraft and vice versa.

One of the mercs was a man named Steiner, a professional soldier for hire. Originally a young warrior in the Wehrmacht in WWII, at the end of the war he had been given the option of soldiering for his French captors in the Foreign Legion or spending an indefinite amount of time interned behind barbed war in a POW camp. He chose the Legion, and later during his service in that fighting force often cursed himself for making the wrong choice. When his term of service was up, he went freelance, and had spent the last three decades soldiering for pay in the world's hotspots. The Congo, Rhodesia/Zimbabwe, Katanga, Cuba (first as an anti-Batista rebel; later, when Fidel went Red, as an anti-Castro guerrilla), Laos, Vietnam, Egypt, Iran, Iraq, Angola, and lately, Panama, El Salvador, Honduras, and Nicaragua.

When night came there was nothing to do in camp but get drunk and listen to each other's bullshit stories. Tracker drank moderately and listened plenty, since there was no telling when a stray scrap of information might come in handy someday. Steiner didn't talk much, but once or twice when he'd tanked up on too much schnapps he'd loosen up and do some talking.

One story he'd told had stayed in Tracker's memory. It had happened back in the late Sixties, during the Nigeria-Biafra civil war. The predominantly Ibo people of Biafra had sought to secede from the parent country of Nigeria, with horrifying consequences on all sides. The Ibos had put up a desperate fight but were outgunned and outnumbered by the Nigerian forces. Nigeria blockaded the province, cutting off all outside food supplies and creating a deadly famine, and in the end the Biafrans had had to capitulate.

It was the worst kind of civil war, with atrocities multiplying on both sides as the combatants sought to outdo each other in frightfulness. The hapless civilians who were trapped in the middle suffered the most, as usual. Steiner had been serving with a crack unit of elite mercs who'd been hired by the Nigerian government, which could better afford such luxuries as expensive foreign fighting forces. But Steiner's unit had earned its pay on many commando missions deep into Biafran territory. Some of the things they did there would have qualified as war crimes if the news had ever leaked out. But it didn't, and besides, Steiner argued, or rationalized, the enemy had done the same things.

Another auxiliary unit working in the same sector, and nominally on the same side, made even the cold-blooded professionals of Steiner's outfit unnerved by their presence. It was a ragtag band of irregulars recruited from the coastal provinces and unleashed on the hapless Ibo villagers. The group was lightly armed and even more lightly provisioned, but they had an extraordinary ability to live off the land. They had an even more extraordinary ability to spread sheer, stark, unrelenting terror in the enemy populace.

"Zey were a bonch of focking *maniacs*," Steiner had said, looking up from the campfire, his pale eyes glazed.

The irregulars were sent in when the commanders wanted a village wiped out in such a way that the horror of it would paralyze the entire district. They struck at night. Sometimes they massacred towns, other times they slew only single individuals. There was no apparent rhyme or reason to their campaigns except that they were designed to kill. The nameless band lived to kill. Indeed, they had a religious obligation to do so.

Major Kwame, a Nigerian officer who was the liaison with Steiner's group, had once told him the secret of the nameless band. All its members were initiates of the Leopard Society. The Leopard Society was a secret cult that had existed in West Africa for hundreds, perhaps thousands, of years. The Leopard was its totem animal, its guiding spirit. The cultists sought to emulate the leopard by killing as the leopard does. Lurking in lonely places, along trails, they would waylay travelers, pouncing on them and killing them with a clawlike metal hand weapon. Sometimes, to nerve themselves up to the attacks, the cult executioners would take a potion, whose main ingredient was taken from human intestines. This would augment their courage and predatory ferocity.

Later, at the end of the war, when the Biafrans had been starved and crushed, Steiner heard another story about the unit of Leopard Men. Apparently they had been the subject of a dispute among the top Nigerian military brass. Some of the generals had wanted to execute all the members of the unit as a public service now that they weren't needed for the war effort anymore. The debate had gone back and forth, resolving itself only when a few of the leading proponents of the extermination faction found claw-shaped amulets placed on their pillows deep in their well-guarded strongholds. The brass paid the nameless unit a bonus, thanked them for their services, disbanded them, and let them disburse to their homes.

Such was the story that Steiner had told Tracker one night in the mountains on the Nicaraguan border.

A year or two after that, Tracker had heard a story about Steiner, that the veteran merc had run afoul of the Panamanian dictator in a drugs-for-guns deal. Steiner had cheated the general's torturers at the last by biting down on a suicide pill that was part of the standard operating equipment for covert operators in the field.

"But I never heard of the Leopard Men operating in this hemisphere," Tracker said.

"No reason why you should have," Captain Martel said. "What have such things to do with you?"

"You'd be surprised. Like I said, I'm part-Sioux. I know about warrior societies, and power medicine, and the totem spirits of animals that enter and guide wizards and vision-questers.

"At second hand, that is," he added hastily, not wanting to fuel Bouchard's paranoia about him. "My grandfather told me stories about such things when I was a boy," Tracker explained.

"Then perhaps you are not entirely without understanding in such matters. But the average American, with your super-highways and computers and shopping malls, knows nothing of these things," Martel said. "Here in the islands, it is different.

"Most of the slaves who were brought to this part of the Caribbean were originally from those West African countries. From generation to generation, the oral history of their ancestral homeland was passed on, and no history of the area would be complete without the *Egbo*. A few initiates of the cult kept the tradition alive in a more direct manner, but it never really took root on these shores. Here it is vodoun that rules, not *Egbo*.

"Forget your Hollywood fantasies of human sacrifice, black magic, and zombies. There is an element of that in vodoun, it is true, a very small element, for there are devil-worshippers everywhere, among all the peoples of the world. But in the main vodoun celebrates the beneficent powers of good, not evil. Like human sacrifice and zombies, *Egbo* lurks in the shadows of the true faith of vodoun.

"But this latest outbreak is different. What I have been seeing—and fighting—here for the last few years is a sinister conspiracy with quite worldly aims. Briefly put, it is a plot by certain unscrupulous individuals to use the trappings of the Leopard Society to create and motivate an army of criminals," Martel said.

"It wouldn't be the first time somebody tried to mix religion and murder. That goes back to the Hashashin of Alamut, the original Assassins, who gave the breed their name," Tracker said.

"Precisely, M. Tracker. And if you know of the Assassins, you know that their master, who sent them forth on their holy missions of murder, was an evil genius known as the Old Man of the Mountain."

"So I've heard."

"Then you will understand me when I say that while the existence of the new Leopard cult is known to me in its general outlines, the identity of its Old Man of the Mountain remains a mystery."

"I wish you all the luck in the world in finding him," Tracker said. "But this sure takes me far afield from my case."

"Does it? I wonder," Martel said. "Consider this: your case has its origin somewhere outside these isles."

"True."

"The weapons being supplied to the cult also come from outside these islands."

"You think there's a connection between my murder case

and these guns? Could be," Tracker said, "but I don't see it yet."

Tracker didn't see the roadblock coming, either.

The road south ran straight across the top of the ridge for four or five miles before reaching the downgrade. This was due to the cliffs of the palisade, whose sides were so sheer that it was impossible to build any roads on them. The descent from the summit couldn't begin until the broken, irregular slopes of the Jambles, whose terrain allowed a switchback road with hairpin curves to be built that linked the ridgetop with the foothills of the lowlands.

The view from the switchback road provided many spectacular scenic vistas, but few drivers were able to enjoy them as they negotiated the sharp turns and the sudden blind curves. There were no guardrails, either, and no lights.

The terraces near the bottom were dotted with the rusting hulks of wrecked cars. Every few months, some driver went off the edge. Once the cars reached bottom, there wasn't much to salvage, so the wrecks were left to rot away.

In most places, the road was so narrow that only one vehicle could travel on it at a time, but on the long straightaways between the curves, the road had been widened, leaving space so that one vehicle could pull over on the side of the road to let another vehicle pass.

The station wagon reached the downgrade without incident and began its descent. The first slope was steep.

There wasn't much talk going down.

Cressy gripped the steering wheel tightly in both hands and all but stood on the brake. The car was in low gear, but that didn't seem to matter much. As it swung around the first curve, there was a dizzying instant as sheer emptiness loomed on the right side.

The sun was low, almost touching the sea, but the surroundings were more brightly lit than they had been atop the ridge, where the bulk of the cliffs blocked the sun.

Far below, the city of Port-aux-Frères could be seen, a cubist assemblage of white-washed blocks that were houses and triangular-shaped wedges that were tiled roofs. A few lights were starting to come on, not many, for Tambour was not rich, and its citizenry did not like to pay for electricity to light their lamps when there was still light to see by in the sky. Those of them that had electricity.

Squealing sounds came from the brake pads as the station wagon poked its way down the switchbacks. Nobody spoke. They didn't want to risk distracting the driver from a job that demanded concentration above all.

There was some relief, but not much, when the car finally reached the middle slopes. A fall from 350 feet will kill you just as dead as a fall from 800 feet.

The car rounded a blind curve that put them on the longest straightaway of the middle slopes. A pickup truck was parked on the side of the road, its nose pointed uphill, its engine idling. The driver was a toothless old man in a ragged wide-brimmed straw hat and a soiled white long-sleeved shirt. The passengers in the car knew he was toothless because of the big friendly smile he gave them as they rolled by. He was still smiling even though a pair of gun muzzles were pointing at him. The guns were in the hands of Captain Martel and Bouchard, who had him covered as soon as they saw the truck.

For once Tracker had been taken by surprise, with no warning notice of the truck's presence. The blind curves and multiple twists and turns of the course threw off his radar-ranging pulses, dissolving clear images in a chaos of radar echoes that made a true reading impossible.

He turned his infrared imager on the truck when he saw it, though. The engine, hot from the climb, blazed like the sun. The image of the man in the cab was a pale shadow compared to that.

The hot engine threw off Tracker's readings, too. The overheated engine registered so brightly that it tended to white-out the big picture. He couldn't be sure if the pickup's driver was alone. He wouldn't have seen any others if they were skulking behind the truck's front, shielded by the engine compartment.

The guns didn't seem to disturb the old man, who just kept

smiling and waving as if it was the most ordinary thing in the world to be passed by a car full of guns pointing at him.

The car rolled to the far end of the straightaway, where the road dipped and made an acute turn in the opposite direction, leading to the next level of straightaway.

That's when they saw the truck. It wasn't a pickup truck, either. It was a big ten-ton truck with a powerful diesel engined. Black smoke puffed from the stack. Gears jammed, crashed, and whined as it muscled its way up. Behind the cab was a flatbed with rail-fence sides. Inside the hopper was a gang of men armed with guns.

They started shooting.

Spearblades of light flared from the muzzles of their weapons. Mostly rifles, with a few machine guns. These guns weren't silenced. They blasted away uninhibitedly.

Cressy hit the brakes. The downtilting car pitched forward so suddenly that the passengers were almost tumbled forward out of their seats. Inside the car, shouting and general confusion.

The truck bulled to the end of the straightaway and started up the bottom of the steep grade. The car was at the top. The angle was so steep that the gunmen were shooting over the top of the car, but they'd soon correct that.

Cressy threw the car into reverse and stepped on the gas. The car surged backward, fishtailing in reverse on a wild ride. Cressy couldn't see very well because there were too many people blocking his view of the rear window.

Metal scraped rock, a tooth-gnashing clangor, as the car veered too close to the rock wall and sideswiped it. Cressy steered away from it, still giving the vehicle plenty of gas to get away from the truck. The car backed onto the previous straightaway, while the truck was climbing the steep curve below. For an instant, they were spared the fusilade of gunfire.

Cressy overcompensated in trying to steer away from the rocks and went too far in the opposite direction. The terrifying emptiness of the void rushed toward the rear of the car. The passengers shouted. Cressy whipped the wheel in the opposite direction, just in the nick of time to keep the car from going over the edge. The right side wheels left the pavement and rode over the ground beyond the pavement's edge. Spinning wheels slewed up a spray of pebbles and dirt. The spinning wheels caught, held, and got some traction, allowing the car to be steered away from the brink.

The front of the truck suddenly appeared around the curve, climbing to the straightaway. It had a massive reinforced steel bumper and radiator grille guard that looked like a piece of armor plate. It could scrape the car off the road like a hockey stick sweeping a puck across the ice.

A bullet shot out the car's left headlight. Another slug knicked the top of the windshield and shot off a three-foot strip of chrome trim. The windshield disintegrated as a third slug tore through it. Safety glass dissolved into a hail of crystal cubes, peppering the occupants of the car like birdshot.

Shouting, Cressy threw up a massive forearm to protect his face, his eyes. He drove blind for a heart-stopping interval.

Tracker didn't have to worry about going blind. He *was* blind. And the polycarbonate composition visor could take a direct hit from a bullet without shattering. The shock of impact would probably kill the wearer, but the glasses would be intact, presenting a headscratching problem for whatever coroner had to examine them. But broken glass was nothing, nothing it all. Some of it sleeted against Tracker's face, marking it with superficial scratches.

Glass cubes bounced off the visor, not leaving the ghost of a mark. Tracker could see perfectly. He could see that the car was steering straight for disaster. He grabbed the steering wheel and turned it so that the car was traveling straight along the middle of the road. It was going backward, but at least it was in a straight line.

"I've got it!" Cressy said.

Specks of glass beaded his face like diamond chips on brown velvet. But his eyes were okay, undamaged. Tracker relinquished control of the wheel and Cressy took over.

A wordless shout from Bouchard alerted them to the next

peril. He was looking out the back and was the first to see that the rear exit had just been closed.

The pickup truck had not been idle during the mêlée. It had gone to the opposite end of the straightaway, where the road narrowed just before curving upward around a mighty shoulder of rock to make the next hairpin turn. The pickup truck was parked broadside across it, completely blocking the way. The trap was now sealed at both ends.

The toothless driver with the straw hat and white shirt was still smiling, but this time he had a gun in his hands. So did his two partners, who must have been hiding in the pickup truck after all. They were younger men, and they weren't smiling, but they had guns, too. All three were standing on the far side of the pickup, using it for cover as they opened fire on the car advancing toward them in reverse.

One of the young men had a bolt-action rifle, and the other had a lever-action rifle. The old man had a pair of six-guns, big .44 long-barreled revolvers, and he was blasting away with them like an oldtime movie cowboy. Each shot from the .44 sounded like a cannon blast, but luckily the car was still too far away for any accuracy with the handguns.

The young riflemen might have been more dangerous, but they barely got off a round or two before Bouchard opened up on them. He cut loose with the machine gun, firing out the back window, spraying a stream of lead in their direction. He couldn't do much in the way of aiming due to the car's erratic evasive movements, but the machine gun spat out so much lead that some of it was sure to score.

The youth with the bolt-action rifle and the pistol-packing oldster ducked for cover behind the pickup's hopper. The other youth stood behind the front of the vehicle. He was working the lever of the rifle when a burst of machine gun fire stitched him across the chest.

Tracker was trying to shoot at the driver's cab of the big ten ton truck, but it was no good; the car was weaving so much that he couldn't make any of his hits count.

The car slowed as it neared the pickup. The big diesel truck started to speed up, whining into higher gear to accelerate on the straightaway.

Tracker grabbed the door handle. "If this doesn't work, butt the hell out of that pickup and you just might clear the road," he said.

"What?" Cressy asked.

"This!"

Tracker yanked the door handle like he was working a one-armed bandit and jackknifed the door opened. The pavement slid by as he dove sideways out of the door, holding the machine gun in one hand.

The car had slowed but it was still a shock to hit the hard roadway surface. Tracker took most of the impact on his shoulder. It was a jarring blow, rocking him. He rolled and tumbled to lessen the shock. At that, he left a couple of square inches of skin on the road to mark his trajectory. He stopped a few feet short of the brink, his head ringing.

Rock chips stung his face and hands, gouged out of the pavement by the bullets the gunmen in the back of the truck were shooting at him. But he lay flat, prone, and the truck was too close to him for the shooters to get the angle.

There was the smell of burnt rubber, oil, rock dust, sweat, and gunpowder. The engine roar from the oncoming truck was a physical presence, as much felt as heard. The pavement trembled from its approach. The massive front wheels tilted toward the right, and the truck followed. The driver intended to run over Tracker!

In the station wagon, Bouchard squirmed headfirst out of the back and into the back seat. Martel and Jack Lashbrook grabbed him and pulled him forward as the car hurtled rearward toward the pickup truck. Cressy was steering straight for it, backward.

The old man with the pistols and the young rifleman stopped shooting and turned to run, too late. There was a bang, a crash, a dull hollow crumping sound as the rear of the station wagon collided with the pickup. Metal folded, accordioned. Glass broke.

The car rocked on its foundations, receiving a tremendous jolt. Its occupants were tossed around the inside of the car. Cressy took a brutal blow across his massive chest when he struck the steering wheel. He hit it so hard that he cracked it.

But his seatbelt was fastened, saving him from serious injury. A ruggedly built individual, he took the impact on his powerful chest muscles, seriously bruising them but not breaking anything.

Bouchard, Lashbrook, and Captain Martel were tossed around in a tangle of flailing arms and legs.

The rear of the station wagon was far more solidly built and reinforced than the side of the pickup truck. Its side panels were punched in. The two wheels on that side left the ground as the vehicle tilted and overturned. It rolled over on the old pistolero and the young rifleman, pancaking them.

The big diesel truck bore down on Tracker, picking up speed. The driver meant to swerve over to the side to flatten Tracker, then keep on going to ram the station wagon.

Firing from the prone position, Tracker poured a mass of lead into the left front tire. It was a heavy-duty truck tire, not easily ruptured, but the steady stream of bullets punctured the massive treads, ventilated them, shredding them. The tire ripped into black vulcanized streamers and came apart. With the tire gone, the vehicle suddenly pulled toward Tracker's right, swinging wildly off course.

Tracker caught a quick glimpse of the driver as he frantically wrestled with the steering wheel, whipping it hard over in the opposite direction to bring the vehicle back on course. The truck ran out of road first. Peeling off at an angle, it sailed off the brink into space. The rear wheels encountered emptiness. The diesel engine suddenly sounded twice as loud as before, now that it no longer competed with the thrumming noise of tires on pavement.

The expression on the faces of the gunmen in the back of the truck was priceless . . . to Tracker, anyway. They had done their best to kill him but he had managed to turn the tables. Now they were on a long swift drop to oblivion. Some of them jumped out of the truck, but it was too late for that ploy to do them any good. Others just held on tight and screamed on the way down.

The truck's descent was a parabolic arc that terminated when it hit an outcropping of rock about 150 feet down. That's when the screaming stopped, too.

The truck accordioned to half its normal size, flipped, and cartwheeled down the jagged foothills before crashing to a halt on its back. Fire broke out, igniting spilled diesel fuel from the ruptured fuel lines. A moment later, the blaze touched off the main store of fuel in the tank, triggering a tremendous explosion. A long column of black oily smoke rose from the conflagration, climbing into the darkening sky.

9.

"Looks like your prisoners are unavailable for further questioning, Captain," Tracker said. "Unavailable this side of Hell, that is," he added.

"And Hell on earth is what they got for their last few moments of life," Martel said. "Not that their crimes didn't merit such a fate, but still, it closes off that line of investigation."

Vachon and Sidiri, or what was left of them, were still smoldering in the center of the town square.

The main administrative and government buildings of Port-aux-Frères were grouped around a plaza on a low hill overlooking the harbor. There was the courthouse, the jail, the mayor's office, and the various ministries of the bureaucracy.

The square was now mostly deserted, although a number of bystanders stood clustered on the sidelines, in the shadows.

Night had come. The sky was full of stars. Street lights with quaint, old-fashioned ornate wrought-iron stands shed a warm amber glow over the square, a soft romantic haze.

Earlier, an angry mob had stormed the jail, overpowered the guards, dragged Vachon and Sidiri from their cells, doused them with gasoline, and set them on fire. Burning is, after all, the most efficacious method of destroying those who are in league with the Powers of Evil.

It was all over by the time Tracker and company had happened on the scene. A crowd was still gathered around the grisly remains, but it broke up fast as soon as Captain Martel was seen entering the vicinity.

That the gendarmes and Tracker had made it back to town was in itself little short of miraculous. They had survived the deadly ambush on the ridge road without any of them sustaining major injuries.

The station wagon, like its occupants, was battered and bruised but still able to keep on going. The rear was pushed in, with the back bumper hanging at a tilted angle. The rear axle was bent, but not so badly as to render the car inoperable. The windshield was no more, having been shattered into crystal cubes of safety glass by enemy bullets. Slugs had punctured the car body in a number of places, but had missed hitting anything vital.

Lines of pain etched Cressy's stolid face. His chest was stiff and sore, a massive bruise where it had hit the steering wheel. It hurt when he drew too deep a breath, but nothing was broken. Captain Martel was bruised and battered from head to toe. Jack Lashbrook had a broken nose and two black eyes.

A bullet had creased the fleshy part of Bouchard's buttocks while he was scrambling out of the back of the wagon just before it crashed into the pickup truck. A nasty flesh wound, it was painful but not serious. It hurt his pride as much as anything else, since there was something ridiculous about being shot in the ass, a fact that only deepened his already foul humor.

Tracker was bruised, battered, stiff, and sore. Much of the skin of his forearms, elbows, and knees had been scraped raw when he jumped out of the moving car.

On the whole, it was not a happy crew that endured the rough ride as the ailing car crawled downhill and limped back into town. On the other hand, they could take some consolation in the fact that they had come out of the attack in considerably better shape than the opposition, who were dead to a man.

That was too bad, in a way, because Captain Martel would have liked to have taken some live prisoners for questioning. Still, despite the pain of his bruises, he had taken the time to examine some of the attackers, or what was left of them.

The toothless oldster with the two guns was relatively intact from the waist up, although the rest of him was squashed flat under the overturned pickup. His ragged straw hat lay upside-down on the pavement, not far from his body. A gust of wind blew up and swept it over the edge of the cliff.

A clutching hand and part of an arm protruded from under the edge of the pickup to mark where the youth with the bolt-action rifle had met his fate. The other rifleman had fallen clear of the pickup, but there wasn't enough of his face left to make an identification. It had been shot off.

As for the others, most of them had crashed and burned with the truck, although a few cadavers had been flung far and wide and were scattered among the foothills and hollows at the base of the slope.

Captain Martel had ordered the car stopped there, so he could get out and peer into the faces of the more accessible corpses. He stretched his arm across Bouchard's shoulder for support. Shock had numbed his injuries, allowing him to overcome the pain and continue to function.

Creaking and groaning, the car had resumed its journey through the lowlands, poking along the winding road to the coast. Night had fallen as the car straggled along the last mile into town, steam hissing from underneath the dented hood. The hot cyclops eye of the single unbroken headlight sent a long lone white beam probing the narrow cobblestone streets of the town below the administrative plaza on the hill.

Few people were abroad on the back streets, and those who were shrank back into doorways or ducked into alleys as the car approached. They didn't know that it carried the police captain and his associates. Apparently they were keeping clear of it as a matter of caution. The massacre had caught the villagers in a grip of fear, and they were avoiding all others who could not be immediately identified as friend or foe.

Or so Martel thought. He and the others knew nothing of what had happened in town during their absence. The first sign of trouble came when the solitary headlight played across the whitewashed walls of the jail.

The outside lights, clustered in corners under the eaves, blazed brightly. They were set to switch on automatically by an indoor timer. But the inside of the building was dark, and some of the windows were broken.

The laboring car slowed to a crawl as it entered the alley between the jail and an adjacent building. A figure stumbled into view at the head of the alley, reeling in the glare of the single headlight. It was a uniformed man, one of Martel's officers. He was hatless and armed with a handgun, which he was waving about. Fighting to stay on his feet, he squinted through the bright light washing over him, trying to make out the occupants of the car.

"Don't shoot—it's Ledoux!" Cressy said.

Tracker held his weapon trained on the newcomer. After Octave, he wasn't taking the loyalty of any of the gendarmes for granted.

Hearing his name spoken, Ledoux lurched toward the car.

"Ledoux! It's me, Cressy!"

Ledoux pointed the gun at the car. There was a metallic *snick* as Tracker released the safety of his gun.

"Don't," Captain Martel said, putting his hand on Tracker's shoulder. Seated in the back seat, Martel leaned forward, stifling a groan of pain the movement had caused him. "Put down your weapon, Ledoux! I, Captain Martel, command you to do so!"

"*Capitaine!* Is it really you?" Ledoux cried.

"Put down the gun, you idiot, unless you want to be shot."

"It's you," Ledoux said. He let his gun hand fall to his side. On rubbery legs, he made his way to the driver's side of the car. He held onto the roof with his free hand to keep from falling over. Blood stained the front of his shirt. "*Mon Dieu*, what has happened to you?" he said, as he realized the extent of the damage to the car.

"No matter," Martel said. He spoke through clenched teeth. The numbness was beginning to wear off from his bruises, and he was starting to feel real pain.

Ledoux leaned down, looking in through the driver's side window. An ugly gash was opened up in the top of his head. Blood from the wound had run down his forehead, painting the side of his face.

"What happened to *you*?" Martel said.

"Octave . . . it was Octave," Ledoux said.

"Him again!"

"A crowd gathered outside the jail—a mob. They wanted the prisoners. Octave . . . he hit me with something when I wasn't looking . . . knocked me out. He shot Henri."

"The devil! Is he dead?"

"No, but he's . . . not good. He's inside. Octave shot him, then he opened the doors and let the mob in. He unlocked the cells so they could get at the prisoners . . . I didn't come to until after it was all over. Henri . . . told me what happened."

"It was just you and Henri? Where are the rest of the men?"

"They were called out to investigate a case of theft. A truck was reported stolen at the construction site for the new dock, out at the cape," Ledoux said.

"So! Now we know where the truck came from that our friends used to try to run us off the road," Martel said.

"What?" Ledoux asked. "Who—"

"Some of our old friends, the Ashfield Boys. The gang from Crapaud's Club Chaudron. They got the worst of it, I am happy to say. There won't be many of them at the bar tonight!"

Ledoux said, "I never thought those jackals would dare to attack the law, Captain!"

"Things are coming to a boil, Ledoux. They thought they smelled blood and were emboldened to make their move. They didn't know that the blood they smelled would turn out to be their own. Most of the gang was wiped out in one stroke!"

"Well, at least something good has happened, then. Was Crapaud among the dead, I hope?"

"I can't be sure, Ledoux, but I very much doubt it. The Toad is not one to risk his own neck unless he has to," Martel said.

"But go on with your story," he told Ledoux.

"There's not much more to tell, Captain. Luc, Chauvin, Ney, and Fouquet went out to investigate the complaint. You know how important the new dock is to our island," Ledoux said.

"Yes, yes. Go on, man," Martel said.

"Almost as soon as they went out, Octave came in. He said that you had ordered him to come in while the rest of you stayed out at the murder house to lay a trap for the killers. About ten minutes later, the mob showed up. They had been drinking their fill in the waterfront taverns and had brought plenty of rum along with them. They were in an ugly mood. They said that no one was safe while devils like Vachon and Sidiri were alive. They demanded that we surrender the prisoners to them."

"Who were the ringleaders, Ledoux?"

"I don't know, Captain. That is, I saw them but I didn't recognize them. Most were strangers to me, but it looked like the loudmouths who were stirring up the trouble belonged to the construction crew working on the new dock. There were plenty of the local drunks and idlers, too, but they stayed mostly in the background."

"The construction crew! What were they doing in town instead of at the site?" Martel asked.

"I don't know, *mon capitaine*."

"So they stopped working early, and the truck was stolen from the site while they were here in town? Most convenient!"

"Henri and I locked up the building at the first sign of trouble," Ledoux went on.

"We were prepared to make a fight of it. I was going to unlock the armory to get the shotguns when Octave hit me from behind. That's all I remember. When I awoke, the cell doors were open, the prisoners were gone, and Henri had been shot!"

"And Vachon and Sidiri? What of them, Ledoux?" Martel asked.

"In—in the plaza, Captain. They were *burned alive*!"

Later: "I just hope it *was* Vachon and Sidiri who got torched, and not a couple of ringers who were switched for them at the last minute," Tracker said.

"It was them," Henri said. He lay on a padded wooden bench, trying to raise himself up on one side, straining from the effort. "I looked out the window when I heard the screams," he said. "It was them. They were screaming even before the fires were lit . . . and for a long time afterward." Exhausted, he slumped back on the bench, groaning.

"Easy, Henri. Don't try to talk," Cressy said. "Save your strength. We've sent for a doctor. Easy . . ."

Henri had been shot in the belly, low on the left side. A bloodstain as big across as a melon marked the wound. A thick pad of gauze bandages was lightly taped down over the bullet hole and had soaked up a good deal of fresh blood.

"The bleeding is slowing," Bouchard said.

"Stupid of me to get shot . . . I saw the gun in Octave's hand, didn't think anything of it, even though it was pointing at me . . ."

"Don't talk, Henri. Rest," Cressy said.

"Even after I was shot, I didn't think he had done it," Henri went on. "I thought the bullet had come from outside, through the window. . . . I couldn't believe Octave had done it. . . ."

"Easy—"

"I—it's better to talk, Cressy. Takes my mind off the pain. It wasn't until I saw Octave unlock the cells so the mob could get at the prisoners, that I knew what he had done . . . that he had shot me. He had to. I would never have given them up to the mob—" Henri fell silent in mid-sentence. His tensed muscles slackened, and his eyes rolled up so that only the whites were showing.

"Henri!" Cressy said.

Bouchard leaned over the wounded man, pressing his fingers against Henri's throat.

Cressy said, "Is he—?"

"No! No, I can still feel a pulse. It's weak, but it's still there," Bouchard said. "And he's still breathing. He must have passed out. He's still alive."

"Where is that doctor?" Cressy said.

He slapped one big fist into his palm as he paced the floor. It was the most emotion Tracker had seen him show since they had first met, early this morning when Tracker showed up at the police station to establish his bonafides to the authorities. Hard to believe that that was less than twelve hours ago!

Even when they had been fighting for their lives, the big constable hadn't shown so much as a crack in his stony demeanor.

"They are cousins," Captain Martel said to Tracker in an aside. "Cressy was the one who got Henri to join the force," he added.

Cressy went to the front of the station, to one of the windows.

"Cressy! Don't show yourself in front of the window, man," Captain Martel cautioned. "There might be snipers waiting outside."

"Yes, sir," Cressy said.

Standing at one side of the window, he lifted the edge of the curtain and peered around the edge of the window frame. Broken glass shattered from the window panes by brickbats flung by the angry mob crunched under his feet.

"I don't see him," he said. "Where's that doctor?"

"It's too soon, Cressy. Luc and Chauvin only left here a few minutes ago," Martel said. "They couldn't have reached the clinic yet, much less returned with Dr. Gaudet."

Cressy turned away from the window, his face angry. "We can't even contact them to see how they're doing, not with the radio smashed," he said.

The two-way radio behind the dispatcher's desk in the front of the station had been wrecked, smashed beyond repair. "I'll bet that was Octave's doing, too," Cressy said. "When I get my hands on that traitor, I'll wring his neck like a chicken's!" His hands looked as big as catcher's mitts as he reflexively clenched and unclenched his fists.

Ledoux said, "Octave must be insane!"

"Worse than that," Captain Martel said. He started to say more, faltered, then winced in pain.

Tracker put out a hand to steady him. "Better take it easy yourself, Captain. You aren't in good shape," he said.

"And wouldn't you know it?" the police captain said wryly.

"Yes, you must not strain yourself, sir," Cressy said.

He walked Martel to a chair and helped ease him down into it.

"Thanks, Cressy."

"It's nothing, sir."

"This injury has taken more out of me than I thought," Martel said. "Damn the weakness!"

"You'll be fine, sir."

"There's a bottle of brandy in the top drawer of my file cabinet, Cressy. Get it, will you? We could all stand a drink right about now," the captain said.

"Yes, sir."

Cressy started for the offices in the rear of the building.

"It's in the space behind the back of the files, Cressy," Captain Martel called after the constable.

"So that's where you keep it!" Bouchard said. "No wonder I could never find it!"

"That's why I'm the captain and you're only a corporal, Bouchard. After tonight, I'll have to find another place to hide it," Martel said.

Cressy vanished into Martel's office, emerging a moment later with a liter-sized bottle of fine old brandy. He stopped to take a look at Henri, who was still unconscious. "How is he?"

"No better," Bouchard said, "but no worse, either."

Jack Lashbrook started to rub his eyes with his hands, forgetting that they were both blackened. The slightest touch reminded him, causing him to jerk his hands away from his face as if they had been scalded. "Christ!" he said. He shook his head sadly. "I'm all fucked up," he said. His voice was funny, because of the broken nose. It made him sound as if he were congested from a major head cold.

"You can put in for a Purple Heart, Jack, or whatever the State Department gives to its personnel when they get wounded in action," Tracker said to him.

Lashbrook took it well enough. "You know what really hurts? When I took the assignment to this post, my boss told me that this was easy duty," he said.

"If you can still joke about it, there's hope for you yet," Tracker said.

Cressy handed the bottle of brandy to Martel, who took it with his good hand. The captain lifted it to his lips—it was corked.

"I'll get that, sir," Cressy said.

"I'm not completely useless, man," Martel said, waving him away. He bit down on the cork and worked it out of the bottle and spat it out. "We won't be needing that again," he said. "And I did that without spilling a drop. I'm not ready to be put out to pasture yet!"

He tilted the bottle and took a long pull of the brandy. "God, that's good! Here, Cressy, take some yourself and pass it around to the rest of the fellows," he said.

"Yes, sir."

Cressy barely touched the stuff, only wetting his lips with it. Ledoux made up for the constable's lack of enthusiasm, drinking hard.

"Hey! Leave some for the rest of us, you pig," Bouchard said, only half-joking. Instead of waiting for Ledoux to pass it to him, Bouchard took it out of the other's hands. The corporal uptilted the bottle and drank deeply. Lowering it, he wiped his mouth with the back of his hands and smacked his lips. "*C'est magnifique!* Now I know what I've been missing," he said.

"Don't get too fond of my brandy, Bouchard," Martel said.

"It's too late, Captain. Now that I've had a taste of the real stuff, I'm a confirmed convert to your brand!" Bouchard raised the bottle for another swallow, caught sight of Tracker, scowled, started to take a drink, then stopped, frowning. Abruptly he thrust the bottle toward Tracker. "Here," he said, "I suppose you've earned your share of this, too, *Americaine*."

Tracker took the bottle from him. "Thanks, that's mighty sociable of you, Corporal," he said.

"Bah! Hurry up and drink it before I change my mind!"

Tracker saluted him, bottle in hand. "Here's to justice," he said, then took a swallow. "There's still a mouthful left, Jack," Tracker said.

"Are you kidding? I feel like I'm going to puke as it is," Jack Lashbrook said.

Bouchard was quick to snatch back the bottle. "Here, give me that!

"To justice," he said, before draining the bottle to the last drop. He hurled it against the wall, breaking it to bits. "And death to the Leopard Men!" he cried.

10.

"WHAT'S THIS NONSENSE about Leopard Men?" asked Dr. Gaudet. He had entered the police station just as Bouchard was making his bottle-smashing toast of vengeance. He was short, plump, neat, and coolly self-possessed. Balding, with a horseshoe-shaped band of curly salt-and-pepper hair above his ears and the back of his head. He wore glasses and a neatly trimmed chin beard that looked vaguely pharaohnic.

The fiftyish black physician was clad in a long white doctor's coat and a light blue high-collared medico's tunic and trousers. He carried a black doctor's bag in one hand.

He was accompanied by a tall blond woman. She, too, wore a long white coat. In her mid-thirties, she was slim, athletic, yet provocatively rounded at the bust and hips. Her hair was pinned up in a knot at the back of her head. It was bronze-colored, with gold highlights. She had a high fore-head, sharp cheekbones, and finely formed features. Wide gray-green eyes, cool and intelligent, contrasted with a mobile, sensuous mouth. She held a boxful of medical sup-plies against her chest.

The newcomers were escorted by the two gendarmes who had picked them up at the clinic and brought them back to headquarters. Chauvin was big, beefy, sloppy, and unshaven. A swollen paunch strained the bottom buttons of his shirt, spilling over his gun belt. Shrewd eyes belied his careless appearance. Luc was in his late twenties, tall, gangling, with the grayish-brown complexion of a freckled shark. Neat as a pin, he wore his sidearm Western-gunfighter style, low on his hip so that his fingers just brushed the gun butt, with the holster tied down on his leg.

They and two other gendarmes made up the team that had gone out to the construction site where the new dock was being built at Cap du Requin, "Shark Cape," to investigate the stolen truck. They had taken statements from the few people present at the scene, most of the crew being absent in town, for reasons that the lawmen would not learn until later. The virtual abandonment of the site had been a godsend to the thieves, who had managed to make off with the truck without being seen by the project boss, foreman, or the handful of guards whose responsibility it was to patrol the sprawling site.

The officers were surprised, and not pleasantly, by their inability to contact headquarters by radio as they returned to town. They were greeted with the news that Groux was dead, Octave was a murderous traitor, Henri had been shot, Captain Martel and his party had narrowly escaped death by ambush, the station had been stormed by a lynch mob, and the prisoners had been put to death in the civic square.

As if all that was not enough, telephone service was out throughout the island. The lines were dead. An ominous development in light of what had happened and what might happen yet.

Captain Martel had sent Luc and Chauvin to fetch the doctor from the clinic. Ney and Fouquet were the other half of the foursome who had gone out to Shark Cape. Captain Martel sent them to fetch a different kind of doctor. They had not yet returned, but Luc and Chauvin had.

Dr. Gaudet tsk-tsked over the broken bottle. "Things are bad enough without you playing the fool, Corporal," he said.

Bouchard winced, looked away, then set his jaw defiantly forward.

"On the contrary, Doctor, he has expressed the sentiment of us all," Captain Martel said.

Dr. Gaudet did not reply. He had already caught sight of

Henri stretched out unconscious in his own gore on the bench, and was rushing toward him. "Lord, Martel, this looks like a war zone!" he said.

"That it is, Doctor—the eternal war of good versus evil."

"Yeah, and so far today, the good's been taking its lumps," Tracker said. "Not that we didn't get in a few licks on the bad guys."

"And the night is young," Bouchard seconded.

"That's what I like to hear," Chauvin said. "By God, we're not going to win any battles by sitting around feeling sorry for ourselves!"

The woman cast a quizzical glance at Tracker as she bustled in, trailing in the doctor's wake. "Where do you want these supplies, Doctor?" she asked.

"Set them nearby," he said, not looking up from his examination of Henri, whom he stood beside on one knee.

The ground floor of the station was divided into three sections: the desk area in front, administrative offices in the middle, and the detention area in the rear.

In front was the duty officer/dispatcher's desk, which was more like a judge's bench. It stood against the wall to the left of the main entrance. The top was eight feet tall, with the floor of the well inside it raised high so the duty officer could look down on all who came into the station. The duty officer's job was the same as the desk sergeant's in an American police station. He kept the log, manned the phones, and dispatched officers to handle complaints. On the side of the desk opposite the front entrance, there was a half-door and three wooden steps.

The two-way radio was on the side of the well opposite the half-door, or would have been, if it wasn't lying smashed to pieces on the floor.

On the other side of the room opposite the duty officer's desk was an ordinary desk where routine paperwork was done. A swivel chair on rollers was behind the desk. One of the rollers was missing. A straightbacked armless chair stood beside the desk. That was where the complainant sat. A few more chairs identical to the complainant's chair were grouped around a nearby table.

A long wooden bench with a thinly padded seat cushion stood against the wall, behind the table and chairs and between the desk and the front door. This was the bench where Henri now lay.

A waist-high wooden divider stretched across the back of the room, running the length of the floor above five feet in front of the wall opposite the main entrance. A hinged gate stood in the center of the divider, opening onto a corridor connecting to the admin area and the detention cells.

The woman in the white coat set the medical supply box down on the desktop. A pocketbook with a long strap was slung over one shoulder. She took it off and laid it on its side on the desk.

Dr. Gaudet took a small packet from the box, unsealed it, took out a pair of rubber gloves, and snapped them on his hands. He made a quick inventory by eye of the contents of the supply box. "We'll need all of these, and more besides."

"There's more supplies in the police car, Dr. Gaudet," the woman said. "I'll get them."

"Please," he said.

He went back to work on Henri. She started toward the door.

"One moment, if you please, Mlle. Flagler," Martel said.

"Yes, Captain Martel?" she said.

"I would prefer you to remain inside rather than expose yourself to further risk."

"I'm in no risk, Captain. The car's just outside."

"We are all at risk, mademoiselle. My men will get the supplies."

She nodded acquiescence. "As you wish, Captain."

Martel sent Luc and Chauvin on the errand.

"You should not have come here, Mlle. Flagler. It is too dangerous," Martel told her.

"I had to. Dr. Gaudet needs an assistant and there was no one else we could spare from the clinic without leaving it understaffed. That would have been dangerous for the patients. Besides, I've been helping out at the clinic for so long that by now I'm a pretty good nurse," she said.

"So you're Kirsten Flagler," Tracker said.

She turned her cool appraising gaze on him. "And you must be this Mr. Tracker that I've been hearing so much about," she said.

"That's me."

"I understand you've been assisting Captain Martel in investigating those dreadful murders at the château."

"Hardly. It's the captain's show. He's been good enough to let me tag along as a kind of unofficial observer."

"Really? Wasn't there enough crime in the States to keep you busy?"

"You could call this a busman's holiday, Miss Flagler. I thought I'd work on my suntan while doing some sleuthing."

"Perhaps my sense of humor is somewhat lacking, Mr. Tracker, but I don't think that the violent death of human beings is a fit subject for joking."

"Laugh or cry, it makes no difference to the dead. They're still dead," Tracker said.

Luc and Chauvin came back in, laden down with cartons of medical supplies. They set them down near the doctor.

"How's Henri, Dr. Gaudet?" Cressy asked.

"Not good, not good. He's in shock, lost a lot of blood. But it could be worse. It looks like the bullet passed through his side without hitting any vital organs."

"We didn't think he'd make it if we tried to take him to the clinic."

"You did well not to. He might have bled to death if he'd been moved."

"Will he . . . will he pull through, Doctor?"

"Not if you keep looking over my shoulder, breathing your germs on him! Lord, Cressy! Go away and stop bothering me, man!"

"Yes, Dr. Gaudet. I will. Sorry."

Kirsten Flagler wanted to treat Martel's bruises, but he told her to take care of the other men first. He sat ramrod-straight in an armless chair against the wall. His face was ashen. A sheen of sweat shone on his creased brow. Chauvin hovered over him.

"What the devil are you doing hanging about, Chauvin? If

it's brandy you're after, you're too late. It's gone and there's no more," Martel said.

"It's not that, Captain," Chauvin said.

"Well, what is it, then?"

"I forgot to tell you . . . Luc and I ran into Valentin and Necker before, when we were bringing back the doctor and Mlle Flagler." Valentin and Necker were two more of Martel's men.

"Where are they now, Chauvin?"

"They were coming back from that job you sent them on this morning, Captain, whatever that was."

"What did they find out?"

"I don't know, they didn't say."

"Why didn't they come back with you?"

"They went to round up some of the boys that are off-duty, Captain. With the phones out, the only way to reach them is to go to their homes in person and roust them out."

"Damn! I need that information I sent them to get!"

"We need men, Captain."

"I need that information more!"

Chauvin looked dubious.

"We've got a hell of a fight on our hands," he said.

"Idiot! You can't fight the enemy until you know who it is," Captain Martel said.

"What about the Ashfield Boys? The Club Chaudron crowd, I mean."

"They're through, Chauvin. Finished. There's not enough left of them to fill an ashtray."

"They tried to ambush you on the road."

"They're hired guns. At least, they *were*," Martel said. "I believe they were hired at the last minute to try to stop me. They're shooters, not schemers. This whole operation is too big for them."

"Their chief, Crapaud, is no dummy. And you said yourself that he's probably still alive," Chauvin pointed out.

"The Toad doesn't have the international connections or the capital to broker an arms deal like the one that's flooding this island with machine guns."

Chauvin scratched his head and ass. "There's the construction crews," he said. "The foreigners. From what I hear, they were behind the storming of the jail."

"Hirelings," Martel said dismissively.

"They've got a lesson coming. We've got to break heads and shoot some of them to teach them not to go against the law."

"You may get your wish, Chauvin."

Chauvin cheered up at the prospect of imminent violence. "There's something fishy about that stolen truck story. It was too pat. I had the feeling that the project big shots were giving us the runaround, Captain."

"Ah," Martel said, "there you may have something, Chauvin! Still, I remain convinced that the matter I assigned Valentin and Necker to investigate is the key to the case!"

"Want me to radio them, Captain?"

Martel pointed at the wreckage of the big two-way set strewn about the floor. "I doubt you'll get very far with that," he said.

"I meant the radio in my car," Chauvin said. There was a stunned look on the captain's face. Chauvin was concerned. "Captain? You okay?"

Martel slapped his forehead with his palm.

"No, Chauvin, I am not 'okay.' The pain must be affecting my brain for me to not think of that. So obvious——! A thousand pardons, *mon vieux*."

"My car's right out in front," Chauvin noted helpfully.

"Then go to it, by all means. Radio Valentin and Necker. Ask them what they found out during their investigation today. Tell them I said they should tell you. When you have the answer, return immediately and tell no one but myself."

"Yes, sir, Captain."

"What are you waiting for, you big ox? Go, hurry! *Vite, vite!*"

"Yes, sir!" Chauvin went.

Dr. Gaudet labored over Henri. Bouchard stood to one side of the bench, holding a desk lamp so it shone down on the patient so Gaudet would have more light to see by.

Dr. Gaudet checked Henri's heartbeat and respiration. He cut off the wounded man's clothes in the area of the injury so he could get at it. The bleeding had slowed to a trickle. He probed, cleaned, and dressed the wound. It was a temporary patch job but it should hold until Henri could be moved to the clinic.

Kirsten Flagler assisted him. She handed him instruments as needed, bottles, bandages, antibiotics.

Finally Dr. Gaudet rose, stretching, trying to work some of the kinks out of his neck and back. "I've done all I can for this man now," he said. He wanted to treat Martel next.

"I can wait. Take care of Ledoux's head," Martel said.

Dr. Gaudet was too tired to argue with Martel and didn't bother to try. He went to work on Ledoux.

"Hi, Kirsten," Jack Lashbrook said.

He'd been sitting off on the sidelines, nursing his broken nose, snuffling, keeping out of the way.

Kirsten Flagler stopped in mid-stride and stared at Lashbrook. "Good heavens, Jack! What have they done to you?" she asked.

"I'm all right," he said. "I got off easy compared to some of the others."

"You poor boy!"

"I've been playing a man's game today," he said.

Chauvin came back in, out of breath.

"Well?" Captain Martel demanded.

"I haven't been able to reach them yet," Chauvin said.

"And you came back in here to tell me that—!"

"No, no!" Chauvin said quickly.

"What, then?"

"Duclos is here, with a couple of men!"

"Good! Send him in, then go back to that radio and don't return until you've reached Valentin and Necker!"

"Yes, sir!"

Chauvin went out as Duclos was coming in. Duclos was a gendarme assigned to the night shift. He had a pear-shaped face, pop eyes, jug handle ears, and a wide down-turned slitted mouth. He bore a strong resemblance to a grouper fish.

He wasn't alone. He'd brought his two brothers and an uncle. The kinfolk were civilians but they were tough men.

They were armed with hunting rifles and a shotgun. All of them bore the same fishy family resemblance.

Duclos himself was in uniform and wore his regulation police sidearm. He also carried a pump-style riot shotgun. He saluted Martel. "Valentin and Necker came by my house and told me what's up. I hurried over as fast as I could, even though it is my day off."

"Most commendable of you, Duclos," Martel said dryly.

"My brothers and uncle came along. They can shoot, too."

"Excellent. Did Valentin or Necker give you something to pass along to me?"

"Huh? I mean, no, sir. Were they supposed to?"

"Damnation!"

"Uh, excuse me, sir?"

"Never mind, Duclos. Glad to have you aboard, damned glad. And your family, too."

"Thank you, sir."

"Report to Cressy and he'll assign you to your posts," Martel said.

"Yes, sir."

As the Duclos clan went off in search of Cressy, the uncle asked his nephew, "When do we get to shoot somebody?"

"Soon, soon," Duclos assured him.

Kirsten Flagler went to Captain Martel, a long pink pill nestled in the palm of one hand. The other held a tiny paper cup filled with water. "This is for you, Captain," she said.

He eyed the pill suspiciously. "What is it?"

"A painkiller. It will help you relax and make you feel better."

He shook his head. "I don't want to relax and I don't want to feel better."

"Doctor's orders," she said.

"Please don't take that tone with me, Mlle. Flagler."

"Why, what tone is that, Captain?"

"The one you're using right now, talking to me as if I were a difficult child who won't take his medicine."

"You're a difficult *patient* who won't take his medicine," she corrected.

"No pills," he said. "I have to keep my head clear, my wits sharp. I can't afford to dull my senses right now."

"It's just a very mild sedative," she said. She was still smiling, but starting to sound just a wee bit exasperated with his obtuseness. "You're not setting a very good example for your men," she said. "They take their cue from you. If you won't take your medicine, they won't either, and some of them need it a lot more than you do. Particularly the more seriously injured. They could suffer grave setbacks without the proper medication."

"Who are these men? Show them to me, and I will *order* them to to take their pills!"

"That's not the point, Captain. I'm talking about you."

"Ah, but it *is* the point, Mlle. Flagler. I am not my men. They are the subordinates, but *I* am the commander. Their leader. I cannot lead them properly unless my mind is as clear as a bell and as sharp as a tack."

"It's not polite to argue with a lady, Captain—"

"There is no argument, mademoiselle. The subject is closed."

Kirsten Flagler heaved a great long-suffering sigh. "I wish I had you as my patient at the clinic," she said.

"Heaven forbid!"

"And I will, Captain, if you don't start taking proper care of yourself!"

"As soon as the present crisis is resolved, Mlle. Flagler, I will be more than willing to take all the pills, potions, and nostrums in your pharmacopoeia. But until then—no!"

"I see I've met my match in stubbornness," she said.

"Pertinacity, I believe is the term," he said.

She put the pill and the water-filled paper cup down on the seat of the chair beside him. "I'll leave this here in case you change your mind," she said.

Captain Martel started to protest, thought better of it. "*Merci*, Mlle. Flagler. I appreciate your concern," he said.

"You're quite welcome. And now, if you'll excuse me, I have other duties to attend to," she said.

"Of course. I fear I've already kept you from them for too long."

As she walked away, she couldn't resist a parting shot. "Imagine, a big brave captain scared of an itty-bitty little pill!" She shook her head in amazement at the perversity of human folly.

When she was gone, Martel reached for the pill and picked it up. The motion jarred him, making him gasp in pain. When the spasm passed, he held the long pink pill between thumb and forefinger, studying it thoughtfully. "I wonder . . . after all, how much worse could it be than the pain?" he said to himself, musing aloud.

Tracker had been following the byplay between the police captain and the would-be caregiver. "Remarkable woman," he said.

Martel started. He studied Tracker's face, which was as unreadable as ever. "Remarkable indeed," Martel said. "The clinic would not exist without her tireless support and patronage."

Reaching a decision, he slipped the pill into his breast pocket. "I can always take it later if I need it, I suppose," he said.

" 'Clear as a bell and sharp as a tack,' eh? Good thing I didn't tell her about your temporary lapse in forgetting that you could use Chauvin's car radio to reach Valentin and Necker in the field," Tracker said.

"A temporary lapse," Martel agreed, "and one which you will not mention to anyone else, least of all the formidable Mlle. Flagler. That is an order, monsieur. You will recall that you are still deputized, and as such, a member of my staff and subject to my orders."

"Don't worry, I don't go around talking about official police business to civilians, Captain."

"A wise policy."

"Anyhow, I don't think she likes me."

"Mlle. Flagler is a humanitarian. She wants to save lives."

"Hey, me too. That's what I'm all about."

"Yes, M. Tracker, but you kill people."

"The ones who deserve it. What the hell, a surgeon's got to cut out the cancer to save the patient."

"An idealist like Mlle. Flagler can have but little sympathy or understanding for your pragmatic viewpoint, monsieur."

"I didn't hear you complaining when I was liquidating the bad guys, Captain."

"Of course not. But then, I am a pragmatist, too."

Tracker changed the subject. "Speaking of official police business, Captain, how about letting me in on the secret of this hot lead you've got Valentin and Necker running down?"

"I will tell you," Captain Martel began. He looked around to see if anybody was listening in. The only other person in the immediate vicinity was Jack Lashbrook, and his only interest seemed to be in nursing his broken nose. Nevertheless, Martel pitched his voice to a low, confidential tone while moving his mouth close to Tracker's ear. He began again. "I will tell you, monsieur—"

He broke off as Chauvin once more entered the building, his piggy eyes hot and bright, his unshaven jowls quivering with excitement. He hurried toward his chief, hitching up his gun belt and holding up his pants to keep them from falling down. He was bursting to tell what he knew. He also burst two buttons off his shirt with his heaving, straining belly. He had rushed in from outside so fast that he was out of breath and couldn't speak for a moment. Red-faced, hacking and coughing, he put a hand against the wall to steady himself while he recovered.

Martel stared at a spot on the ceiling and fought to control his impatience.

Chauvin's entrance was noted with interest by Jack Lashbrook. His eyes glinted, narrow slits in bruised purple pockets. "What's up? Must be something big to get Chauvin moving that fast," he said.

"Never you mind about that," Kirsten Flagler said. She stood beside him. He was sitting down, looking up at her.

"Christ, I must look like a real mess," he said.

"Language, Jack, please!" she said, sounding faintly scandalized.

"Uh, sorry."

"I forgive you because I know how uncomfortable you

must be, dear. I've got something that will make you feel better."

"I'll say."

She waved a chiding finger in front of his swollen face. "Don't be crude, Jack. You know how I feel about off-color remarks, especially when they're made in public."

"You know how I feel about you."

"Silly boy." She held out a long pink pill and a paper cup of water. "Setting that broken nose of yours is going to be a very painful process," she said. "And it was such a cute nose, too."

"Gee, thanks."

"Don't be grumpy. I'm sure it'll be even cuter when it's fixed. But that won't be for some time."

"What's the pill?" he asked.

"A painkiller."

Interested, he picked it up off her outstretched palm. "Is it strong?" he asked.

"No more than the recommended dosage."

"I hope it's strong. I'm hurting."

"It's good for what ails you. But it won't work unless you take it. I hope you're not going to be as difficult about taking your medicine as Captain Martel was," she said.

"Not me. I can't resist your bedside manner."

"Naughty, naughty," she teased. She handed him the paper cup. "You can wash it down with this," she said.

"Okay, nurse." Jack Lashbrook started to open his mouth, grimaced, then shuddered. "Damn! It even hurts to open my mouth," he said.

"The little pink pill will fix that. That's what it's for."

He parted his jaws, placing the pill on his tongue. Tossing the water back in his mouth, he gulped down the pill.

Kirsten Flagler watched to make sure that he swallowed it. "That's a good boy," she said. She ruffled his hair. "You know, Jack, I'm really quite fond of you."

"You know how I feel about you, Kirsten." He reached for her but she eluded his embrace, laughing softly. "Kirsten . . ."

"I really must go, Jack. I've got others to take care of. Now you just sit here and relax and think of me."

"You're all I do think of, Kirsten."

"Sweet," she said. She patted his cheek.

"Oww," he complained.

"Did that hurt? Poor baby, what a bruising you must have suffered."

"I'm hurting all over."

"My little pink pill will do away with all your aches and pains. In a few minutes, you won't feel a thing."

"I sure hope so."

"I guarantee it," she said. "Bye now."

"Bye."

She crossed to the far side of the room.

Jack Lashbrook watched her. He loved to watch her move. Not that she strutted her stuff or anything obvious like that. That wasn't in her nature. She couldn't do an ungraceful thing. But the way she carried herself, she was like a dancer. A ballerina. A prima ballerina.

Heads turned in his direction. Tracker, Captain Martel, and Chauvin were all looking at him. Staring. Had he spoken aloud by mistake? Maybe he had, he wasn't sure. That pill was sure coming on strong. He was rushing out from it. He reminded himself to be careful not to lose control, to say or do anything silly. Where was Kirsten? He looked for her but didn't see her. His eyes were having trouble focusing. When he squinted he could see better. A flash of gold caught his eye. Her hair. It stood out in a crowded room.

She was leaning over the desk, reaching inside her pocketbook for something. Or maybe she was putting something away. That must be it, she was putting something away, because her hand was empty when she when she withdrew it from her bag. She fastened the clasp, making sure it was tightly shut, then placed the pocketbook carefully on its side on the desktop.

She went around behind the desk to the wooden divider at the far end of the room. She put her hand on top of the hinged gate, pausing to look back over her shoulder. She was looking at him! She smiled and blew him a kiss. Then she pushed open the gate, stepped through it, closed it behind her, and disappeared into the dark corridor of the office area. He leaned forward, craning for another glimpse of her, and almost fell off his chair. "Christ, I must be really zonked!"

That's what he said. Or thought he said. Or had he just thought it, and not said anything? He must have said something, because all at once a wall closed in around him, a living wall, a wall of hard-faced men with angry eyes and loud, accusing voices. Accusing him!

Shaking his head to clear it, he fought to make out what they were saying, to resolve the babble into distinct and separate voices. *There* was one he knew—Captain Martel's! No mistaking that deep, resonant, basso profundo voice with its flawlessly articulated diction laced with exotic Caribbean music.

What was Martel saying . . . ?

"John Lashbrook, I arrest you in the name of the law, for conspiracy to commit murder!"

11.

CAPTAIN MARTEL WAS coming on strong. It was the kind of situation that every crimebuster worth his or her salt dreams of; the classic set-up where the cunning sleuth unveils the killer before a room full of admiring witnesses. Now it was Martel's turn, and he was pulling out all the stops.

Jack Lashbrook must have sensed that the game was up. He started to fall apart at the seams when Martel took the first step toward him to arrest him for murder. Even before that, he didn't look too good. He could barely sit still while Martel was getting the damning facts from Chauvin, who had gotten them by radio from Valentin and Necker, still out on the road. Too bad they weren't here to see how their leg-work had helped cinch the case against a killer.

Chauvin told what he had heard. Tracker listened in, saying nothing, his face a mask of perfect neutrality. When the facts were in, Martel went to get his man. Tracker and Chauvin followed close behind.

Jack Lashbrook reeled under the inexorable oncoming tread of the Law. He almost fell off his chair. Martel's hand shot out, grabbing a handful of material at Lashbrook's shoulder, lifting him back into his seat, holding him in place while the police captain delivered the damning indictment. Martel said, "You were very clever, M. Lashbrook. You played your role of the naïve male ingenue to perfection. For a time—a short time, but still, a time—you even had me believing in your innocence. But you forgot one thing, monsieur: the police deal in facts, not appearances."

"Huh?" Lashbrook said.

"You are the Judas, M. Lashbrook, the Trojan horse, the false friend who wormed his way into the Slawson household so you could deliver them all to a cruel and violent death. It was you who arranged the subterfuge with the keys to the alarm switch-box.

"You entered the Slawson home on the afternoon before the murders. You have been there before, a number of times. That is fact, not supposition. Your position as consular assistant requires you to make the rounds of the social scene. Since M. and Mme. Slawson were also Americans like yourself, you had many opportunities to visit their house as a guest.

"On that fateful afternoon, I imagine the scenario went something like this: You, the charming guest, find some reason to absent yourself from your hosts. You go to the alarm box. The key is in the lock, as was the custom. You open the box, make sure the alarm is off, lock the box, remove the key, and substitute the wrong key in its place, working it in deep so that the lock is jammed. It could all be done within two to three minutes, less time than it takes to use the facilities to answer a call of nature—which, I suggest, might well have served as a pretext for you to excuse yourself from your hosts.

"Your part in the crime is done. Perhaps you were only a dupe of your as-yet-unknown masters, unaware of the deadly purpose which your little subterfuge had furthered. It is pleasant to think so, but that is for the courts to determine. As for the higher-ups, they shall not long escape me. Even now, the net of the law tightens around them, until soon they shall be snared, just as you now are," Martel said. "What have you to say to that, M. Lashbrook?" he asked.

"You're crazy. I didn't go to the house that day, and I didn't have any reason for killing them," Lashbrook said.

"Your own guilt betrays you, monsieur. Look at yourself. You are so distraught that you can barely frame the obligatory protestations of innocence. Your face is flushed. You slur your words like a drunkard. You are all but falling out of your chair."

"I was in a car crash today, remember? You should, you were there," Lashbrook said.

Martel's lips quirked in a bitterly sardonic smile. "I expected you to cite that in your own defense," he said. "I wondered about that myself. Why would M. Lashbrook, who I believe is part of the murder gang, risk his own life by running the gauntlet of ambushers on the return to town?"

"Yeah—why?"

"Because you had no choice. You were playing with fire when you used the evil cult of the Leopard Men to do your killings. Such fanatics are not to be controlled. When they learned that I had found the sacred claw, they didn't care who they had to kill to get it back. You see, *Egbo* ritual demands that the claw be present at the scene when a Leopard Man kills. And so it was at the château, but the unexpected happened. A simple thing, really, but because of it many would die, may yet die.

"The cord broke. That is all, monsieur. The cord broke. The cord which held the claw secured to the person of one of the cult executioners, the *Bati Yeli*, no doubt the chief *Bati Yeli* of the group. For want of a cord, the claw was lost. For want of the claw, the cult was prepared to risk all. To send three of the killers back to the scene of the crime the next night, daring all odds to recover it. But two of them were caught—Vachon and Sidiri—and the *Egbo* received its second setback.

"For want of the claw, the cult dispatched three more executioners to secrete themselves where they could spy on the château day and night, beyond the range of the alarms, standing watch so that if the claw was found by a nonbeliever, they would be ready to act, to kill. But that was not all. They even had an agent planted among the police, in the person of Octave. The cult must have planned that years ago in anticipation of a future need.

"By sheer chance, the claw was found, thanks to my colleague M. Tracker, a man who certainly knows how to keep his eyes open." Captain Martel acknowledged Tracker's contribution with a slight but correct bow in his direction.

Martel went on: "Disaster struck the *Egbo* once more with the finding of the claw. I do not doubt that Octave would have killed us all if he had thought he could have accomplished the foul deed by himself. But he dared not risk the chance of failure. Instead, he set out to alert his masters. Ironically, had he but known it, three very willing and able accomplices were hidden nearby, under his very nose. But he did not know of it. It is not the first time in a conspiracy that the right hand did not know what the left hand was doing.

"Octave killed Groux, stole the car, and raced to alert the cult of the discovery. But time was running out. They were unable to hatch their clever plans. They had to act fast. The telephone lines were already down on Fire Ridge, sabotaged on the night of the murders. Sometime tonight, not long after Octave contacted his masters, the central exchange for all the telephones on the island was dynamited, cutting off communication.

"At about the same time, a truck was stolen, or made to look as if it had been stolen, from the Cap du Requin dock construction site. I will pass over that aspect of the case because it is still under investigation, but I expect that arrests will be made shortly. I find it more than coincidental that while some of my men were decoyed to the cape to investigate the theft, members of the construction gangs incited a riot in town, stormed the jail with the help of Octave, and murdered the two captured members of the cult before they could testify.

"A notorious gang of hoodlums, the Club Chaudron crowd, were hired at the last minute to try to stop me from returning to town. They were transported in the oh-so-conveniently 'stolen' truck, and some of them were armed with the same model of smuggled machine guns used by the *Bati Yeli*. Unfortunately for their plans, some quick thinking and straight shooting by myself and my associates sent the Chaudron gangsters to the same fate which they no doubt intended for us.

"No, the master conspirators—I do not name them *yet*—

have suffered nothing but reversals and setbacks since the *Bati Yeli* lost the claw. All because of a broken rawhide cord. Some might say that it was merely by accident that the thong broke—or was it Fate?"

Martel paused to draw a breath, when he noticed that Jack Lashbrook wasn't paying attention to him. Lashbrook sagged in his chair, limp. His head was tilted so that the back of his skull was propped up by the top of the backrest. His eyes were closed, his face and neck were flushed bright red. His breathing, which was done through the mouth, was heavy, labored.

Martel was irked. He felt like an aggressive salesman whose hot prospect has just fallen asleep in the middle of his million-dollar pitch. He grabbed Lashbrook's lapel and gave him a good shaking. "Am I boring you, monsieur?" he said.

Lashbrook started, somewhat revived. His eyes glittered and his face was feverish. "I feel . . . funny," he said. His voice was a croak. He rubbed his throat and tried to swallow.

Martel was silkily insinuating, "Something is troubling you, monsieur? Your neck? Or is your throat sore? Perhaps it is anticipating the kiss of Mme. la Guillotine?"

"The guillotine!"

"Ah, I thought that might bring you to your senses, M. Lashbrook, or what remains of them, at any rate. Yes, the guillotine. That is how we execute murderers on our little island. A relic of our French heritage. Not as scientifically advanced as your American electric chair, but effective all the same."

"The guillotine!"

With the experience born of countless interrogations, Martel knew that his suspect was nearing the breaking point. He pressed his advantage. "Yes, the guillotine. Mme. la Guillotine has not been used for some time, so doubtless she is a bit rusty, even dull. Do not worry. When the time comes for your fatal rendezvous with her, I promise you that she will be razor-sharp and well-oiled," he said.

Jack Lashbrook writhed as though trapped in the coils of a waking nightmare. "The guillotine? You're mad! I haven't committed any crime," he said.

Martel got ready to play his trump card. "No, monsieur, you are the one who is mad! Not that that will save you from your fate. Our courts do not accept the so-called 'insanity plea.' Because any man is mad who thinks he can defy the law and get away with murder. Just as you were mad *when you used your own car to drive to the château on the afternoon of the murders*!"

Jack Lashbrook's reaction to Martel's final, damning accusation was even more dramatic than the police captain had dared to hope. Lashbrook leaped bolt upright, jumping to his feet, knocking over his chair, his hands balled into fists.

Chauvin started to move in to club him down, but Martel waved him back so as not to spoil the confrontation.

"No! Oh my God, no!" Lashbrook cried.

"Yes, monsieur, yes!"

Martel's face was inches away from Lashbrook's as he delivered the wrap-up like a prosecutor giving the summation in a capital case.

"Yes, M. Lashbrook! Remember that I said that the police are concerned above all with facts, not appearances! My men have been gathering the facts that damn you as an accessory to murder! Acting on my instructions, officers Valentin and Necker have gotten signed statements from no less than three different individuals who are prepared to swear in court that on the afternoon of the murders your automobile was seen entering and leaving the château! Iron-clad testimony, signed, sealed, and sworn to by three unimpeachable eyewitnesses with no other involvement in the case! All three described your car, independent of each other, and one even remembered part of the license number!"

An insistent tugging on the back of Martel's sleeve had been vaguely annoying him for some time during the confrontation, but now it became so agitated that it was impossible to ignore. Glancing over his shoulder, Martel saw that it was Duclos who was so urgently trying to get his attention. Martel jerked his arm free from the other's grasp and waved him away, as if he were shooing away a persistent horsefly.

Like a horsefly, Duclos was not so easily gotten rid of.

"Pssst! Captain! Pssst!" Duclos kept calling to him in an exaggerated stage whisper.

"Not now, fool," Martel said in an aside to the other, speaking out of the corner of his mouth.

"But Captain, this is important," Duclos said.

"Later!"

Jack Lashbrook trembled, as if with fever chills. "I didn't do it," he said, "but God help me, I know who did! It was—AARGHH!"

Jack Lashbrook was suddenly paralyzed, as if he'd been instantly turned to stone. Frozen in the middle of his anguished denial, he stood statue-still, rigid, not moving a muscle. He didn't so much as blink. Caught off-balance when he went inert, he toppled sideways to the floor and lay there, stiff as a board.

Silence.

Chauvin was the first to speak. "Couldn't take it," he said. "Fainted."

Tracker knelt beside the body, searching for signs of life. "Fainted, hell! He's dead."

12.

Martel said, "So, he managed to break his date with Mme. la Guillotine after all!"

"But, Captain—"

Martel whirled to confront the persistent pest. "By damn, Duclos, I hope you're ready to start walking a night beat in the toughest waterfront district in town!"

"This is important, Captain."

"Lord have mercy on you if it's not, Duclos, because *I* won't! Well, man, don't just stand there blinking those pop eyes of yours at me. If you've got something to say, say it!"

"This is hot stuff, sir—confidential!"

Martel allowed Duclos to lead him away from the group clustered around Jack Lashbrook's dead body. "This is far enough, Duclos. Let's have it," Martel said.

"It wasn't him."

"Him?" Martel was puzzled. "Him who?"

"Him! The dead man, Lashbrook. He didn't do it!"

Martel shook his head, more in sorrow than in anger. "I hope that this job that you used to have as a policeman isn't the sole support of your poor family, Duclos," he said.

"I know what I'm talking about, and I can prove it!"

"What are you talking about, Duclos?" Martel said, sighing.

"Lashbrook couldn't have gone up to the château on the afternoon of the murders, because he was in town all day!"

"Ridiculous."

The idea was so far-fetched, so out of touch with reality, that Martel couldn't even find it in himself to be angry at Duclos. He started to turn to walk away.

Duclos blurted, "Ask Father Paul!"

That stopped Martel. "What?"

"Ask Father Paul, he'll tell you!"

Father Paul was the priest of the largest and most important Catholic church in Port-aux-Frères.

Seeing that he had Martel's attention, Duclos talked fast. "Lashbrook had lunch with Father Paul in the rectory, and they spent the whole day making plans for a fundraising drive to restore the church tower and the altar and the stained glass windows," Duclos said.

Martel was tolerant, sympathetic. "That simply cannot be, Duclos. I have three excellent witnesses of impeccable character and no possible involvement with the case who will swear that they saw Lashbrook's car at the château during the middle of the day."

"I don't doubt that it was Lashbrook's car, but he wasn't in it! My brother, Narcisse, was doing some carpentry work for the good father that day, and he saw Lashbrook at the church, too!"

Narcisse Duclos and the other brother and the uncle stood together off to one side, watching Martel and Gendarme Duclos. When Martel turned to look at the other Ducloses, Narcisse nodded his head up and down, signalling yes. Yes, he saw Lashbrook at the church that afternoon.

"I don't ask you to believe simple folk like us, Captain, but surely you'd believe Father Paul, and he'll tell you the same thing," Gendarme Duclos said.

"But if it wasn't Lashbrook driving the car, then who—no, no, something's wrong, it must be a mistake," Martel said.

"Maybe somebody borrowed his car for the afternoon, or took it without telling him and brought it back before he noticed it was missing . . . Did any of your three witnesses actually say that they saw M. Lashbrook? Or did they only see the car and not the driver?"

Martel stroked his chin for an anxious moment. "Who else have you told this to, Duclos?" he asked.

"No one! You always tell us not to discuss official police business with anybody else."

"And your three relatives . . . are they closed-mouthed men, too?"

"To be sure, Captain! They can keep their mouths shut tighter than a clam."

Martel squeezed Duclos' shoulder. "You know, Duclos, I've underestimated you. With a mind like yours, a promotion is a certainty!"

"You're too kind, Captain. But there is one hitch . . . ."

"Eh? What's that?"

"Father Paul. He may feel duty-bound to tell about how he was with Lashbrook."

"You let me worry about Father Paul," Martel said.

"Yes, sir."

"Those brothers of yours look like fine, strapping lads, Duclos. Have they ever considered a career in police work?"

"No, sir, but—"

"Well, let's sleep on it. There are some openings in the department. . . . We'll discuss that at a more opportune time. But for now, mum's the word on what you've just told me, eh?"

"Like a clam, sir."

"Good man," Martel said.

Tracker finished his examination of Lashbrook's corpse and came walking briskly to Martel. He was intent, his brows furrowed over the top of his eye visor. He asked Martel, "Did you take that pill that Kirsten Flagler gave you?"

"No, not yet. Why?"

"Jack Lashbrook did."

Martel wasn't quite sure what Tracker was getting at. "So . . ." he prompted.

"So that's what killed him," Tracker said. The solution had come to Tracker only a moment ago as he was examining the peculiar symptoms of Lashbrook's sudden death. In a flash of intuition he had remembered Steiner, the German merc who had first told him of the Leopard Men. He had also remembered how Steiner had taken a suicide pill to cheat the Panamanian dictator's torturers of their fun.

"What are you trying to say?" Martel asked Tracker.

"I'm saying that if you had taken that pill, you'd be as dead as Lashbrook is right now. Deader. She tried to get you to take the pill first, remember?"

"M. Tracker, I have the greatest respect for your deductive abilities, but in this case, you must be mistaken. I could no more believe that Kirsten Flagler is a poisoner—"

"Than you could believe that Octave was a Leopard Man? Analyze that pill and I'm betting you'll find that it's a fast-acting rocket to the morgue."

Martel looked queasy, rubber-legged.

"You didn't take that pill?" Tracker demanded.

"No, but—I almost did," Martel said, swallowing hard. Fear was replaced by a mounting molten rage. "Why—why would Mlle. Flagler try to poison *me*?"

"I couldn't help eavesdropping on her and Lashbrook while they were talking. Looked to me like they had some kind of understanding, maybe even a relationship. You might want to check on her alibi for the afternoon of the murders, Captain. After all, she's in town most days, working at the clinic. Just from the short time I was watching them, I got the impression that they were close enough friends that he'd let her borrow his car for the afternoon," Tracker said.

"Then—then it could have been Mlle. Flagler who sabotaged the alarm system and set up the Slawsons to be murdered?"

"What could be more natural than a good neighbor dropping by in the afternoon for a little tea and a chat?"

"*Sacre bleu!*"

Martel seemed even more shaken by Kirsten Flagler's possible involvement in the murders than by his own narrow escape from poisoning. He said, "But *why*? Why would she do such things? She's rich, attractive, revered throughout the island for her philanthropic and charitable works. Why would someone with so many advantages steep herself in such evil? What possible motivation could she have?"

"Why did Cain slay Abel?" Tracker continued. "Maybe she just likes to do evil things, the way some people like stamp collecting or marlin fishing. Who knows? We can ask her why when we catch her. And speaking of that, where is she? I haven't seen her around her for the last few minutes."

He looked around the station for her. And when someone with Tracker's powers and abilities looks for a person, he finds that person if he or she is within range of his scopes, screens, and sensors. He didn't find Kirsten Flagler, but he found a little momento that she had left behind to remember her by. "Uh-oh," he said.

"What?" Martel said.

Tracker crossed the room to the desk, where Kirsten Flagler's pocketbook lay on its side on the desktop. He looked into it. He didn't open it, he just looked into it with his computer-generated beams and rays. Inside the pocketbook was a bomb. A live bomb, armed and ticking.

But Martel didn't know that, and when he saw Tracker reaching for the pocketbook, he said, "What are you doing?"

"Shhh. Don't disturb my concentration," Tracker said. "One wrong move, and KA-BOOM."

"What!" It took a second for the realization to sink in, and when it did, Martel's eyes widened and he began backing away.

"And don't start a panic, either. A stampede might set this thing off. Play it cool, Captain."

Captain Martel tried to look nonchalant. He did a pretty fair imitation of a man whistling his way past the graveyard.

Tracker's beam probes had reassured him that the pocketbook wasn't booby-trapped to go off if the catch was opened. He opened it. Inside was a timer, filament detonator, and a couple of pounds of ultra-lethal concentrated plastique explosives. He wasn't exactly a demolitions expert, but he'd spent enough time around high explosives and those who used them to get a pretty good grounding in the subject. The bomb seemed like a simple enough device. It didn't look like it had been rigged to explode if anybody tampered with it.

Of course, it could have been designed by a diabolically clever explosives expert who made it look like a simple device to deceive the unwary into blowing themselves sky high by trying to shut it off.

Start thinking like that, and the terrible ifs multiply until the thinker is too paralyzed by the uncertainties to act. So Tracker didn't allow himself the indulgence of that kind of thinking. He gave it his best appraisal and acted on it. Which was just as well, because the digital timer was ticking away a countdown to demolition.

Tracker switched off the timer.

The tiny greenish-white phosphor digits blanked into nothingness.

A minute passed before Martel spoke. "No . . . KA-BOOM?" he asked.

"We're not strumming harps, so I guess it's safe to say, no KA-BOOM," Tracker said.

Martel let out the breath he'd been holding. He let it out slowly, as if afraid that a too-profound exhalation would trigger the bomb. He sounded like a tire with a slow leak.

Apart from the captain and Tracker, no one else in the station had the slightest suspicion of what had just occurred. "Relax," Tracker said. "We had plenty of time before the bomb was set to explode."

"We did?"

"Sure. At least fifteen seconds."

A quick search revealed how Kirsten Flagler had made her escape. She'd gone into one of the back offices, opened a window, climbed out of it, and lowered herself to the ground. She was long gone.

"I'll find her," Tracker said.

13.

WHEN VOODOO BATTLES *Egbo*, it's Snake versus Claw. . . .

But this was a battle of bullets and bombs, not sorcery and spells. The biggest battle on Tambour since the days of the buccaneers, when pirate navies flew the skull and crossbones, the Jolly Roger, and the dreaded Black Flag that meant no quarter asked or given, a fight to the death.

"That's Mr. Chesterton, the man behind the Cap du Requin project," Captain Martel said.

He started to pass the binoculars to Tracker, who waved them aside. "You keep them. I can see fine without them," he said.

"Yes," Martel chuckled, "yes, I believe you can."

It was night—midnight of the same day that had begun with Tracker climbing into the back seat of a police car early in the morning to take a ride up to the château on Fire Ridge.

A moonless night, but it was still brighter than day, thanks to the colossal conflagration that raged on Shark Cape. Miles south of Port-aux-Frères, the cape was a long crescent-shaped formation that thrust out into the sea then curved around until its tip was pointing back at the shore. A jagged scythe of rock, coral, sand, palms, and scrub brush, it formed a tremendous natural harbor.

Mr. Chesterton and his associates grasped the potential of the site, and had moved to exploit it to the fullest. Thus, the

Shark Cape waterfront development construction project. The project was sited on the leeward side of the cape. Mountains of landfill had been excavated, torn out of the ground. Mighty earth-moving machines loomed over the landscape, rearing up against the sky like primeval metal juggernauts. Pilings had been sunk deep into the sandy bottom of the harbor, rows of them, thrusting far from shore. Sites had been surveyed and marked out for future docks, warehouses, quais, and cargo ship berths.

Mr. Chesterton and his fellow investors had brought in a small army of construction workers. The vast majority of them were wreckers, not builders, a hoodlum army infiltrated into Tambour under the guise of a construction battalion. A goon squad in hardhats. Mr. Chesterton and friends would settle for nothing less than complete domination of the island. That was the best way to maximize profits.

Their scheme for conquest had hit a snag, though. Tonight, the people of Tambour had come to take back their island.

The investors had their own private army. But there existed on Tambour an organized hierarchy whose past stretched back hundreds of years, which could put its own army of fighting fanatics into the field at short notice, so extensive was its reach over every nook and cranny of the island, every cay and inlet, every village and town. And when its long-suffering legions finally rose up in righteous wrath to smite the invaders, it struck like a hurricane.

Vodoun was its name, sometimes known as voodoo.

Hundreds of islanders massed on the cape in the dead of night, armed to the teeth and armored with the unshakable belief that the elemental powers of the earth, air, and sea fought on their side. And one more elemental: fire.

The Cap du Requin shorefront development project was burning, ignited by the flames of hundreds of torches. That was the conflagration that lit up the night. A firestorm, an inferno, a roiling red-lit Hell on earth. Clouds of oily black smoke climbed into the sky, roofing it as far as the eye could see.

The development project's fuel dumps burned hot and

bright. Fiery snakes, hundreds of feet long, writhed across the crowds. The developers' hoodlum army was being given its walking papers by the good citizens of Tambour. They served notice with bullets, bombs, molotov cocktails, machetes, knives, even their bare hands.

It was more than a rout, it was slaughter. A few boats were putting out to sea as a relative handful of the invaders made their escape. Most of them would drown in the treacherous seas before dawn. But the vast majority of the hoodlum battalion would remain to leave their fire-blackened bones on the cape that they had thought would be their beachhead for total conquest.

The outraged islanders had destroyed the main body of the enemy. Captain Martel and his men were going after the head. Tracker was with them.

Mr. Chesterton's stronghold was on the tip of the island. It was a luxurious pleasure palace surrounded by gardens and moats and fountains, even a private zoo. It was surrounded on all sides but one by water. There was a private dock. A gleaming white yacht, some sleek lowslung power boats, and even a propeller-driven seaplane were moored there.

Tambour's voodoo army came by land, but Martel and his gendarmes came by sea, in low, fast cruisers. They waited offshore, dark, silent, unobserved, until a series of explosions at the construction site signalled that the battle had begun. Pillars of fire climbed hundreds of feet high.

Mr. Chesterton had built his forces with money. That was their weakness, their Achilles' heel. When they saw that their cause was lost and they hadn't a chance of winning, the big boss's bodyguards were the first to desert.

Now Chesterton and his inner circle were running for their lives, trying to make their getaway. Their escape route went from the palace, across the pleasure gardens, and then to the marina where the seaplane and boats were secured. It was a short distance from house to dock, not more than a hundred yards, the length of a football field.

There was only one drawback: Martel and his men were dug in in a strong position on the high ground between the palace and the docks.

Chesterton and his cronies came tearing through the gardens, laden down with oversized suitcases stuffed with cash. There was Chesterton himself, four or five of his best gunmen, and another dozen or so mid-grade shooters. And one woman. Kirsten Flagler.

"The bad penny always turns up," Tracker said when he saw her.

Firelight transformed the seascape into a hellish vista, lurid, bloody light.

"Here they come," Cressy said.

Chesterton and his gang were about halfway across the gardens. A heavyset man with slicked-back silver-gray hair held a gun in one hand and a suitcase in the other.

"That's Chesterton," Martel said to Tracker.

Like he said, Tracker didn't need binoculars. He didn't even need his night vision screen, because the firelight provided plenty of illumination to see by. He focused his video eyes on Chesterton, subvocalizing a command to zoom in on the project boss. The man's image filled his inner screens. "Chesterton, hell! That's Carl Chezz," he said.

"Who?" Martel asked.

"Carl Chezz. He used to be a bigtime hood back in the States, a power in one of the most corrupt unions in the world," Tracker said.

"He seems to have graduated to bigger things."

"Tonight's the night he gets his diploma," Tracker said. "He'll finish his education with full honors."

"Eh?"

"He's going to receive the coveted magnum cum laude."

"Ah."

"I plan to bestow the award personally," Tracker said.

Carl Chezz. Now it all fit. It was the last piece of the puzzle that Tracker needed to make sense of a chain of murders stretching from Boston to the boulevards of Paris, from the Hudson River Palisades to the Caribbean Sea.

Martel and his men were positioned behind a waist-high concrete wall on a high pavilion commanding excellent sightlines and fields of fire encompassing the entire estate. Metallic cricketing sounded as Martel's team of crack marksmen readied their weapons to open fire. "Not yet," Martel said. "Not yet . . . let them get a little closer, out in the open, hold your fire—"

Shooting erupted. But it didn't come from the high-powered rifles of Martel's men; it came from the gangsters themselves. Gunfire crackled between Carl Chezz's personal bodyguard of five handpicked gunmen and the dozen or so lower-status shooters. The two sides were blasting away at each other at pointblank range in a vicious firefight. Red tongues of flame stabbed from the muzzles of big-bore handguns. Shots and screams blended into one. A sawed-off shotgun added its dull booming blast.

One of the hoods in Carl Chezz's inner circle was dragging an oversized suitcase across the terrace. It was so heavy that he could barely manage it. The others pulled ahead of him. "Hey, wait up!" he cried.

"I know that one," Tracker said. "That's Mickey Greffle, Carl's number-one boy. He dropped out of circulation about ten years ago."

A shot tagged Mickey Greffle high in the side, spinning him around. He kept his feet and didn't let go of the suitcase, either. A shotgun blast roared into him, ventilating him. The suitcase popped open, raining money. Bricks of hundred-dollar bills spilled on the concrete, a greenback bier for Mickey Greffle, who gasped his last sprawled atop them.

That started a scramble among some of the other hoods for the money. Three died in the struggle.

"We don't even have to shoot," Martel said. "They're killing each other without us firing a shot."

"Why should they have all the fun?" Tracker asked. His question became academic a moment later as the last half-dozen hoods came running toward the gendarmes' ambuscade. Carl Chezz was in the lead. Kirsten Flagler was right beside him. Martel gave the final command. "Ready . . . aim . . . *fire!*"

Martel's marksmen cut loose on the hoods. A withering blast of lead cut them down like weeds.

But not Carl Chezz. He had the devil's own luck on his side. A split-second before the fusillade, he tripped and sprawled face-down. Kirsten Flagler was hard on his heels. She couldn't stop in time and tripped over Chezz before the bullets flew.

Carl Chezz and the woman had fallen below the line of fire, so the bullets tore harmlessly above their heads. A tussle developed between the two. Carl Chezz had dropped the suitcase when he fell. It slid about a dozen feet away from his outstretched grasping hands. Kirsten Flagler crawled over him, reaching for the suitcase. He grabbed her ankle but she kicked free. She grabbed the handle of the suitcase, got her feet under her, and broke to the left, toward the cover of a line of palm trees.

Cursing, spitting, Chezz got on his hands and knees. Maniacal rage distorted his face as he saw the woman escaping with the money. His first shot caught her in the back, knocking her forward. She still gripped the suitcase. His second shot finished her. She threw her arms straight out from her sides and flopped face-down into a reflecting pool. The suitcase popped open, scattering wads of greenbacks across the surface of the water.

Keeping low, Carl Chezz crawled on hands and knees toward the pool, grunting and gasping but still going.

"This one's mine," Tracker said.

Martel motioned to his men to hold their fire.

There was a sudden silence as the shooting stopped. Tracker shouted, *"Yo, Carl!"*

Surprised to hear himself called by a name he had buried along with his hoodlum past over a decade ago, Carl Chezz looked up. Tracker blew his head off.

"Bravo!" Martel said, clapping him on the back. "M. Tracker, I give the highest compliment I know: if you are ever in need of a job, there will always be a place for you among the gendarmarie of Tambour," Martel said.

"That'd be an honor, Captain, but no thanks," Tracker said. "It's too dangerous!"

Later, as the victorious gendarmes made their way back to the mainland, they passed a head stuck up on top of a high spiked fence. Octave's head.

"Now my day is complete," Tracker said.

14.

A MAN WITH a mission made his way through the halls of the Capitol building in Washington, D.C. A man obsessed. He was Leonard Flagler, and he had nothing left to live for. His only joy was in contemplating the manner of his imminent death. He was ruined financially, legally, and emotionally.

Once a titan of industry, his intricate financial scams and schemes had finally come crashing down on his head. What little money he had squirreled away had been used up in paying for his massive legal bills. He had only paid off a fraction of the total. His lawyers had given him the kiss-off, and major jail time was a certainty.

The only person in the world he had ever loved—besides himself—had died a violent death.

A downtrodden, careworn, beaten man, a pathetic figure in a rumpled gray suit, he made his weary way toward his final appointment. He was scheduled to meet with two of the most powerful men in the United States—in the world. One was Senator Hobart Calloway, scion of one of the most illustrious and infamous political dynasties in America. The other was Benjamin Forge, the power behind the Calloway throne. The fixer, the gray eminence, the master manipulator who knew how to get things done, whether it was fixing a manslaughter case in Virginia or a rape case in the Virgin Islands.

Calloway and Forge, the Pol and the Puppet Master. They were firmly established at the summit of political and financial power, elite and untouchable. They had everything, Leonard Flagler had nothing. Well, almost nothing. He still had the final gift given to him from beyond the grave by his beloved daughter, Kirsten. It was in his briefcase.

The Senator and the Fixer thought that Flagler had something that they wanted, that they needed.

Flagler knew the truth about some of the dirtiest deals that had gone down in American political life over the past quarter-century: Presidential assassinations—the Marseilles heroin connections—the savings and loan scandals—bank frauds that had looted millions and destroyed lives wholesale—toxic waste poisoning—hitmen for hire—guns for hostages—drugs for guns—

The dishonor roll of every dirty trick that had stuck it to John and Jane Q. Public.

Flagler knew the truth about the corruption because he had been in on most of it himself, making hay while the sun shone and when it was raining, too. He knew plenty, and would tell plenty. That kind of inside information is better than money, because it's harder to get.

Leonard Flagler was ready to deal. Immunity and a fresh start, and he's spill his guts. That was his proposition, and the Senator and the Fixer would jump at it.

Why not? It's what they would have done if they were in his shoes, which they were damned glad they weren't. He was a drowning man clutching at straws, about to go down for the third time. He would deal. He had to. His other options had all run out.

The Pol and the Puppet Master were the only game in town. Oh, there were plenty of others like them, because the town was Washington, D.C. But none of the others had the clout of this duo. They could offer a marginally better deal than the competition. Marginal, because it was a buyer's market. His bargaining power was almost nil. If he didn't strike while the iron was hot and cut his best deal, he was going to go to jail for the rest of his miserable life, and everybody knew it.

They had to figure that they could get him on the cheap. And so they thought. But they had another think coming. Leonard Flagler had a hole card, an equalizer, an ace up his sleeve that they couldn't possibly suspect.

He knew the truth about them. A man named Tracker had told him. A terrible man, if he was a man. Sometimes lately in the dead of night, Flagler wondered if Tracker even existed at all. His only meeting with the terrible man seemed unreal. Had he hallucinated the encounter? But the thing in his briefcase was real. Kirsten's gift.

"You can't kill me." That was the first thing that Tracker had said to him during their one and only face-to-face meeting.

That had been months ago, before Flagler was completely washed up. He was on the ropes then, but he could still get things done. Like murder. His investigators had learned enough of the truth about Kirsten's final days down in Tambour to be able to tell him something about Tracker. Not much, but enough for Flagler to want to kill him.

He had tried. Three times. Calling on his underworld connections, he had hired hitmen, contract killers, three of the best in the business.

Three failures. It was uncanny and frightening the way each of the assassins had seemed to drop off the face of the earth shortly after picking up the contract to kill Tracker.

And then Tracker had picked him up. Flagler still wasn't sure how it had been done. The last thing he remembered was getting on an elevator in an office building in New York City. He had blacked out. When he came to, he was—where? He didn't know. It was a small square room with gray featureless walls, a gray carpet, a table, and two chairs. He was strapped down to one of the chairs. Hospital-type restraints secured his arms and legs to the chair.

"You can't kill me, so stop trying. You're only wasting my time and your money, and I've got a lot more time than you've got money," Tracker had said.

"Where—where am I?" Flagler asked.

"Nowhere. You've fallen into the crack between the worlds. My time is precious so don't waste it. I've got something you need to know, so shut up and listen," Tracker said.

Tracker sat in a chair opposite him, facing him across the table. He wore sunglasses. Flager could see himself reflected in the lenses. It was eerie, unsettling. Hypnotic. Yes, that was it, hypnotic. Because Flagler had stopped his bluster and bullshit and listened to the man.

"It's a long story so I'll start with the part where I come in. Pay attention, because that's where you come in," Tracker said.

"Once upon a time there was a politician who did something stupid. An innocent girl died because of it. We'll call him the Pol.

"The Pol had a partner who knew who to cut corners and fix problems and didn't give a damn about who got hurt in the process. Call him the Puppet Master. The Puppet Master had a son. He was no damn good. There was something twisted in his head. While the father didn't care who got hurt in the process of fixing things, Junior liked to hurt people. But his father loved him, just like you loved your daughter.

"One day, not long ago, Junior did something really stupid. Big league. It was going to take all the Puppet Master had to square this beef, and maybe that wouldn't be enough.

"Junior's trial was coming up. If he didn't walk out of the courthouse a free man, he was going away for a long time. It didn't look so good for him, because he'd done a lot of stupid things in the past. They'd all been fixed, but if they ever came up in court, there wouldn't be enough fixing in the world to keep Sonny from pulling a long stretch in the pen. That's when the Puppet Master got his bright idea, one that would eventually get a lot of people killed, including your daughter, Kirsten. Not that she wasn't headed down that route anyway.

"The Puppeteer's reasoning went something like this: if the people who'd been problems in the past were fixed permanently, then the past would be fixed, too, because they wouldn't be around to maybe show up in court some day with some damaging testimony that would send Sonny to the slammer. So the Puppet Master decided to fix all those potential problem people, but good. He knew how to pull the strings to get people killed, just like you do, Flagler. But his people were better and gave me a harder time.

"During Junior's college days, he did one of those big time stupid things I was telling you about. He's got a problem: he thinks girls are for hurting, especially the ones who say no. Something happened during winter break at a ski lodge that year. The girl was hurt really bad, worse than the others had been all the other times Junior ran amuck.

"Daddy fixed this, but there were witnesses: Rory Cobbett, Belinda Bates, and Julia Munro. All college kids at the time, rich and spoiled and not too savvy about the way the world really works. But that's ancient history.

"Even further back, there was a woman named Helena Carlton. I think that's when the pattern started, but I'm not sure. She was a good friend of Junior's mom, the Puppet Master's wife. Junior raped her. He was in his late teens at the time. I've seen pictures of her, so I can tell you that Helena Carlton and Junior's mother were lookalikes. Striking resemblance. Make of that what you will.

"Time passed. Junior grew to young manhood. He'd found a pattern he liked, and it worked for him so he kept with it. There were other victims along the way, lots of them, but Junior always got away with it. It's tough bucking one of the most powerful dynasties in the country, especially if you've just been raped.

"Another victim along the way was Alana Pershing. English. Good family, cultured, educated. She had something that the others didn't have, a friend who would one day grow up to be a famous gossip columnist. Maybe you've heard of him—Toby Tamm. Writes a monthly column for a slick mag named *Sideshow*. Smart guy. Does his homework. I got a lot of the background material I'm giving you now from him. He was keeping a low profile for a while back there. People were trying to kill him. But I'm getting ahead of myself.

"Things came to a head when Junior pulled his latest rape. This one was too big to be swept under the rug. This was trouble. So Daddy decided to sweep all the potential problem people under the rug instead.

"The contracts were let and the killings began. They were made to look like accidents if possible, but sometimes that's not always easy to arrange. In that case, the hit was made to look like a random kill, something totally unrelated to the real cause of the murder. It's a simple technique and it works. There's so many killings going down nowadays that nobody can keep track of them.

"Rory Cobbett was shot dead in what was made to look like a holdup. Alana Pershing went out a window. Toby Tamm smelled a rat and went into hiding right after that, which is why he's still around today. Helena Carlton's boat blew up. A French girl, Giselle Durand, killed in a hit and run.

"Then it was Julia Munro's turn to die. Car 'accident.' That's where I came in, for reasons that don't concern you. But when I get on the trail of a crime, I usually get results. This one stumped the hell out of me because I was trying to figure it from a national security angle and getting nowhere fast. That's because it didn't have anything to do with national security, just with saving Sonny from the slammer, and keeping the dynasty's image nicely polished.

"I picked up on the link between Cobbett, Julia Munro, and Belinda Bates, who in the years since college had married a banker named Slawson. Maybe you knew him. They had a couple of kids, too. After Julia's 'accident,' Belinda figured out enough to get scared and took it on the run. That's the one that bothers me the most, because I was only a day or so behind her. If I'd gotten a break, or she had, things would've been different.

"Slawson had a place on Fire Ridge on Tambour. Helluva place—but what am I telling you for? You've probably been there more times than I have. You should have seen the blood.

"It just so happened that the Puppet Master had an in on Tambour, of all places. It was just one of those things, but who knows? Maybe when you get to be that big, you've got an in everywhere in the world. Maybe, but there can't be many ins like Carl Chezz. Thank God. There's one less now, because I liquidated the Chezzman. Maybe you didn't know that, Flagler.

"Carl Chezz was a big time hood about twenty years back. Labor racketeer with one of the dirtiest crooked unions in the country, the Rocky Mountain Mining and Heavy Equipment Operators union. Back in the bad old days, it was bossed by Nicholas J. Nork, Nicky Nork from Newark, New Jersey. Everybody above a certain age remembers him. Say the words 'labor racketeer' and Nicky Nork comes to mind. Crooked as hell, and tough as they come.

"The Pol and the Puppet Master sure have reason to remember him. The Pol made his rep prosecuting Nork. Man, did those two hate each other! The Pol really had a hard-on to send Nicky up the river for life. Which he did, thanks to Carl Chezz. The Chezzman was Nicky's hatchet man, a real stone killer. So mean he made Nicky look like Santa Claus. Nicky didn't massacre the women and children unless he had to, but the Chezzman got off on it. Which goes to show you that people don't change, because Chezz was still pulling that gag right up until the day he died.

"Chezz did something stupid and got caught and was slated for life plus ninety-nine years in prison. Then he got smart. He got in touch with the Puppet Master and offered to make a deal. He'd help the Pol get Nicky in exchange for a get-out-of-jail-free card. It was a done deal. Nicky went to jail, the Pol got plenty of the publicity he loves, and Chezz got to walk away from the raps hanging over him. Everybody was happy but Nicky, I guess.

"The Chezzman's one of your warm weather hoods: Miami, Tampa, New Orleans, Houston. But he was too hot for the States. A lot of people thought the deal smelled. Chezz was a worse hood than Nork ever was, and he got to walk away from a couple of murder raps while Nicky went down on pension fund fraud. J. Edgar Hoover's boys told Chezz in no uncertain terms that he was persona non grata in the USA.

"Chezz went down to the islands and wound up on Tambour. He'd gotten some smarts and lots of big ideas in the last twenty years. He had a beaut of a one about Tambour. Its location makes it a key distribution center for drug smuggling, gun running, and off-shore banking scams. Off-shore banking scams are your line, too, aren't they, Flagler? Quite a coincidence that you and the Chezzman wound up as neighbors on the same island. There's probably something worth looking into there, but not for me. Chezz is dead and you don't look at all well.

"Like I said, Chezz had some big ideas, but this was the biggest one yet. He planned to take over the whole island, lock, stock, and barrel. There was just one obstacle to his takeover plan, but it was a big one, bigger than his big ideas: Voodoo. Or vodoun, as they call it. You hear a lot of things about it, and some of it is pretty wild, but who knows? But one thing you can't get away from is that the religion *is* the infrastructure on a lot of the islands, especially Tambour. Any takeover attempt is going to run into that fact head-on before too long. Vodoun is one of the best-organized resistance movements ever thought of. Don't forget, a lot of those folks are the descendents of runaway slaves, rebels, and pirates, and they are *tough*.

"Chezz found that out fast. He convinced some money men to bankroll the building of a brand-new harbor and port. It would have been a smuggler's dream come true, but why not? The Caribbean has always been a smuggler's paradise and probably always will be. But there was trouble in paradise, and its name was Chezz. The Chezzman was an in-your-face hood, and it didn't take the locals long to find out. Things got so bad that he couldn't get the islanders to work on building his port. I found out why. The vodoun priests put out the word that he was strictly poison.

"Chezz had to bring in outside labor to get his project built. In a way, that suited him fine, because he was able to build up a private army of goons and toughs for his future takeover bid. But the bottom line was that he was a hood from Cleveland muscling in on a tropical island. He was definitely off his turf. He needed an equalizer, something that could go head to head against the vodoun establishment.

"He found it. *Egbo.* Maybe that's a nonsense word to you now, like it was to me before I found out what it meant, but it's some hardcore stuff. Chezz thought he could build up the cult to where it could compete with the vodoun. He was wrong, because it was like trying to make crack troops out of a bunch of homicidal maniacs. Vodoun's a religion, a philosophy, but *Egbo*'s just killing.

"Right while all this is going on, Chezz gets a message from the States. An old acquaintance wants him to take care of some business. Nothing major, it's right in the Chezzman's line: murder. There were probably a hundred different ways to do away with Belinda Bates-Slawson without raising an eyebrow, but Chezz can't be bothered with that kind of stuff anymore. He's a big shot, a would-be conqueror. Besides, he's probably curious to see the cult crazies on his payroll do their stuff. There's one tricky angle, though, a fairly sophisticated alarm system that's going to take something more than hack and slash to get around. The job calls for an inside man.

"Which is where your daughter comes in. I don't know what made her tick and I doubt that you do. If ever there was such a thing as a real-life Jekyll-and-Hyde character, it was her. How do you reconcile the do-gooder who established a free clinic with the murderess who set up a family to be slaughtered? Split personality? I don't know. But she and Carl Chezz were a match made in Hell. Right up to the end, they were trying to double-cross each other.

"Want to hear something funny? The islanders, they still think she was something kind of special. Her grave's like a shrine; they're always putting fresh flowers on it. There's even some kids named after her. Kirsten Flagler's a good name down there. They remember the good deeds, the charitable works. The clinic's still going strong. There's even a movement going around to rename it for her. They think that she was kidnapped and killed by the Chezzman. They don't know about any of the other stuff, like the poisonings, the madness, and the murders. Maybe some of the vodoun priests do, they're pretty smart, but if they know, they're not talking."

Tracker paused then.

"All right," Flagler said. "What's your pitch?"

"It depends on you. On what kind of a man you are. What kind of a father. How do you want your daughter to be remembered?"

"*Damn* you."

"Don't be corny. I'm the keeper of your daughter's secrets. Others know parts of the story, a little bit here and there, but I've got the big picture. If I leaked even a sliver of the truth to the media, it'd be one of the biggest crime stories of all time. Kirsten Flagler would be world-famous, like Lucrezia Borgia or Ma Barker or Bonnie of Bonnie and Clyde. Hell, you've been raked over the coals by the media yourself, so you know how it works.

"Or I can bury the truth and let the world go on thinking that Kirsten Flagler was a gentle, loving person. The world will forget her soon enough, but not the people of Tambour. That way maybe some good comes out of it," Tracker said.

"What do you want me to do?"

"I've seen your doctor's reports. Don't ask me how. I just know how to find out things. I know that you're not long for this world, Flagler, not at the rate that the cancer is eating up your insides. You've got maybe a year, tops."

"What of it?"

"This case hasn't been entirely satisfactory for me. I rolled up lots of the small fry, a few middle-level figures, and one semi-big fish in Carl Chezz. But the real criminals, the ones who set the whole murder carnival in motion, got away scot free," Tracker said.

"I'm no killer," Flagler said. "If you want them dead, kill them yourself. That's your line, not mine."

"I'm not a free agent, Flagler. The people I work for have a strict rule about not interfering in domestic politics. They broke that rule once, a long time ago, and there's been hell to pay ever since. I would act if I could—but I can't," Tracker said.

"My God," Flagler whispered. "Now I know what you want me to do."

"Two men, Flagler. One's connived at cold-blooded murder a hundred times over and gotten away with it. The other's benefitted from his partner's evil and empowered it but prefers to look the other way to keep his 'conscience' clear. Two men, architects of a dynasty of evil.

"You don't have to decide now, Flagler. The life is still strong in you. I'll be watching you. When the sickness has eaten you away to where life is more feared than death, I'll contact you one last time," Tracker said.

Flagler opened his mouth to speak and the world went dark. He woke up in his own bed. Twenty-four hours of his life were missing. The bodyguards who had been in the elevator with him when he was taken sent an urgent plea for him to bail them out of jail. A cop had found them sprawled in a drugged stupor in an alley and had arrested them all for being drunk and disorderly.

That was months ago. Since then, the inroads of his sickness have left Leonard Flagler a hollow man. The life has run out of him like the stuffing from an old torn doll.

A few days ago, Leonard Flagler returned to the shabby single-room apartment where he spends his days and nights counting down his deathwatch.

There were two packages on the table. How had they gotten there? The apartment door had been locked as always when he returned. Two packages, and a sealed envelope that he had overlooked in the puzzlement of the event.

The bulkier package, about the size of a wrapped bundle of laundry, contained confidential dossiers on a prominent political duo. Explosive material, worth a fortune to any news magazine, it documented in chilling detail the crimes and corruption of a dynasty of evil that manipulated American democracy as its own private plantation.

Leonard Flagler arranged for the information to be passed along where it can do the most good.

The second, smaller package was little larger than the lady's pocketbook contained inside it. Inside the pocketbook was something that had belonged to his daughter, along with detailed instructions as to how to use it.

The envelope contained two items. The first was a note printed in block capital letters in pencil:

EVERYTHING IN THE DOSSIERS IS TRUE.

IF YOU WANT TO DO SOMETHING ABOUT IT, SEE THE INSTRUC-
TIONS ENCLOSED WITH THE DEVICE. IF NOT, DISASSEMBLE IT AC-
CORDING TO INSTRUCTIONS AND SCATTER THE PIECES IN THE
OCEAN.

IF YOU SHOULD DECIDE TO USE THE DEVICE, MAKE CERTAIN
THAT IT IS OPERATED ONLY IN THE PRESENCE OF THOSE FOR
WHOM IT IS INTENDED. ANYTHING ELSE WOULD BE CRIMINAL.

NO MATTER WHAT YOUR CHOICE IS, REST ASSURED THAT I WILL
NEVER DIVULGE CERTAIN SECRETS KNOWN ONLY TO YOU AND
ME. YOU HAVE MY SOLEMN WORD ON THIS.

THE PHOTOGRAPH ENCLOSED WITH THIS NOTE WAS TAKEN RE-
CENTLY IN PORT-AUX-FRÈRES, TAMBOUR. THIS IS HOW THE
WORLD SHALL REMEMBER KIRSTEN FLAGLER.

YOU WILL NOT HEAR FROM ME AGAIN.

GOODBYE AND GOOD LUCK.

The note was unsigned.

The enclosed photograph was a snapshot taken on a sunny
day of a clean, new, modern medical facility. Carved in stone
over the entrance was the legend:

KIRSTEN FLAGLER MEMORIAL FREE CLINIC

The snapshot was inside the left breast pocket of Leonard
Flagler's shirt as he proceeded down the corridors of power
to his destiny. His step quickened as he approached the office where he was expected. Inside were two individuals
who were long overdue for such an appointment.

He had made certain that they would be alone, a condition
they agreed to to humor his "paranoia."

Inside his briefcase was an explosive device that could be
detonated by thumbing a simple but fail-safe trigger mechanism built into the bag's handgrip.

The charge was powerful enough to blast a hole in the
Capitol dome, yet shaped to avoid buckling the walls of adjacent offices.

When it detonated, Leonard Flagler did not hear the blast.
But the world did.

WELCOME TO TEXAS, A.D. 2035

Once there was peace and justice in the great state of Texas. There were men of glory who protected the law: they were the Texas Rangers . . .

But the 21st century has spawned a new breed of criminal armed with state-of-the-art weapons. It has also spawned a new breed of lawmen: a rebel force of high-tech avengers hellbent on a quest for justice.

THE TEXAS RANGERS ARE BACK— ### WITH A VENGEANCE

Turn the page for an exciting preview of the new action/adventure series . . .

THE LAST RANGERS

by Jake Davis
Available now from Berkley Books!

1.

A SKY-HIGH SENTINEL stood watch over Texas.

Neither spirit nor flesh, the sentry was a machine made of lightweight high-tensile metalloys, ceramics, racked scaffolds of gridded laser holography crystals, and miles worth of micro-etched printed circuitry. It was crammed with telemetric and communications hardware.

It was *Lone Star Sat*, an eye-in-the-sky spy satellite that floated in geo-synchronous orbit 23,000 miles above the Texas plains. It looked down on an uneasy world wracked by catastrophes both natural and man-made. A hole as big as Ohio gaped in the ozone layer above the South Pole; a smaller hole, Rhode Island–sized, punctured the ozone over the Arctic Circle. Melting polar ice caps had raised the sea level, swamping many of the world's great coastal cities. Turbulence beneath the earth's crust had created new belts of live volcanos, submerged some island chains, and upthrust new ones from the sea bottoms. The recent North Pacific Mega-quake, the long-dreaded Big One, had erased a third of the old California coastline.

The greatest catastrophe of all, though, was the population explosion. People continued to outbreed the planet's capacity to feed them all. The result: a neverending chaos of famine, crime, plague, and war.

Such was the state of the world in the year A.D. 2035.

Lone Star Sat kept on the lookout for dangers that might threaten the great state that had birthed it and lofted it into space. It was the far-seeing and far-hearing eyes and ears of Texas. Arrayed banks of eagle-eyed reconnaissance cameras and electromagnetic signal wave detectors monitored a land mass the size of France. It tracked killer storms in the Gulf, volcanic eruptions in the Vulcan Belt along the Border, cyclonic activity in the Panhandle, tremors in the Ozark earthquake zone.

It also guarded against the potential violence of those who hated Texas, enemies both foreign and domestic who sought to conquer or destroy it. Texas was big, strong, rich, and independent. Her wealth was envied and her maverick ways hated by persons who had less and wanted more and preferred stealing to working for it. The satellite's neutrino spy rays probed the ocean depths for enemy submarines and undersea bases. Its No-Sparrow-Falls space-borne radar net detected unidentified aircraft while they were still well outside striking range; ground-based surface-to-air SAM missile batteries swiftly destroyed them if they persisted in remaining unidentified. Infrared sensors, sensitive enough to detect a match flame flickering on the ground, searched ceaselessly for the telltale heat signature from the exhaust of a hostile missile being launched. Surveillance cameras eyed the movements of navies in the Gulf and armies in Mexico and Central America.

There were other, subtler threats, which the satellite could not see: the schemes of the greedy, the violence of the lawless, the murderousness of ruthless adventures. A band of farsighted individuals had foreseen the dangers, though, and planned accordingly. They had found a champion, armed and armored him as no man had ever been armed and armored before, and sent him on a mission to bring law and order to the wild world of Texas, A.D. 2035.

This is his story.

2.

A CAGEFUL OF crooks settled to the ground in front of the county sheriff's substation in Beamer Junction shortly after sunrise. Beamer Junction was a way station midway between San Antonio, Texas, and Del Rio on the Border. The substation was an igloo-shaped concrete bunker that was buried underground except for its dome-shaped top, a hump that protruded above the surface like a half-buried tortoise shell.

The subterranean command post was manned by a crew of two. Deputy Sheriff Emil Benedict was the senior partner, the man in charge. His subordinate was Assistant Deputy Clem Sugarland. They were monitoring the above-ground scene on the viewscreens of the control panel console. They had been on full alert since the moment the remote sensors first flashed warning of an unidentified airborne being vectored out of the predawn darkness toward the station.

Benedict and Sugarland were in their battle stations. Even an insignificant outpost such as this could defend itself with multilaunch rocket batteries, high-explosive artillery shells, machine Q-guns armed with ion-charged and fragmentation pellets, and electronic warfare (EW) capabilities. The structure itself was hardened against enemies, thick-walled, with the entire central shaft mounted on massive coiled-spring shock absorbers to minimize the concussive impact of a direct hit.

But if the bulky aerial intruder were the spearhead of an attack, it was a ploy unlike any the lawmen had ever seen or heard of. They held their fire as the scanned object's image resolved itself on the screens:

A steel cage filled with what the computerized automatic target recognizer (ATR) identified as "viable bio-units"—that is, live human beings—was being ferried toward the station by a low-flying MagLev suspensor freight barge. Hovering eight to ten feet above the ground on unseen magnetic force fields, the barge drifted stationward with a slow, stately progress not unlike that of an old-time dirigible.

The station was buried in the ground at the northern end of Main Street, which ran north-south. The broad thoroughfare was crossed by the east-west highway connecting San Antonio with Del Rio. The town of Beamer Junction, such as it was, and it wasn't much, was centered around the crossroads. The inhabitants had abandoned the streets at the first sign of trouble, barricading themselves behind the bulletproof shutters and blast-resistant walls of their homes to await the outcome of this bizarre incident.

The suspensor barge glided up Main Street, settling to a landing on the plaza fifty feet away from the station.

"Well, I'll be double-dipped!" Deputy Sheriff Benedict said, staring in disbelief at the viewscreens' multiple close-ups of the hapless prisoners penned in the cage.

"If you're seeing things, then so am I," Assistant Deputy Clem Sugarland said.

"Give us some audio."

Clem threw switches and turned dials, until an exterior directional microphone picked up the clamor inside the cage. A many-voiced torrent of noise came pouring out of the console speaker grids, a babble of bloodcurdling threats and mind-staggering promises of riches. Threats or promises, the ultimate goal was the same: to escape from the cage.

Benedict zoomed in one of the spy-eye cameras to focus on a particular prisoner. A facial close-up of a shaggy-haired, red-bearded giant filled the screen. Glowering from under tufted eyebrows, he sneered with infinite disgust at his fellows and himself.

"My Lord, is that really *Mars Barton*?!"

"Sure looks like him," Clem said.

"Oh my Lord—"

"Looks like he's been in a fight, too. See them powder burns and scorch marks on him? And look at that black eye! Somebody sure pasted one on him to leave him with that big black shiner. Man, I'd sure like to meet the hombre who hung that one on him!"

"Me, too—so I could wring his damn fool neck!"

"Huh?" Clem frowned, puzzled. "I don't get it. Barton's one of the most wanted men in the state—heck, in the whole Southwest, and Mexico, too! He's been getting away with murder for years—"

"Yeah," Benedict said. "Why'd he have to turn up on *my* doorstep?"

" 'Turn up'? I'd say it looks more like he was delivered, served up to us on a silver platter—though how that was done is a mystery to me. Anyhow, whoever done it ain't here to stake his claim, which means that we get to split the reward money. Ol' Mars has got a high price on his head. We're gonna be rich, Mr. Benedict!"

"What good's being rich if you're dead?"

". . . Say again?"

"Barton's been getting away with murder for years because he was supposed to. He's a top hired killer who's laid down hits for some of the biggest names in the state, and I mean B-I-G big, boy. They're not going to sit back and wait for his testimony to put them all in the death chamber. They'll come for him!"

"Shucks, I've been risking my neck on this job just to keep my meal ticket on-line. Reckon I can stand a whole mess of trouble when there's a big payday to be won."

"Big talk," Benedict said. "You'll change your tune when Mars's pals show up here to bust him out. Those killers have weps you never even heard of, ones that could crack this station like an eggshell. This glorified gopher hole wasn't made to hold the likes of him."

"Or nobody else, hardly."

"What the hell's that supposed to mean?!" the deputy shouted, red-faced.

"Don't mean nothing at all, Mr. Benedict," Clem said with an expression of open-faced innocence.

"By Gawd, if that's an accusation, come out and say it to my face instead of pussyfooting around it!"

"You got me stumped, Mr. Benedict, sir. Accusations? About what? You're my boss. What would I accuse you of?"

"Why—why, nothing, of course!"

"Naturally," Clem agreed. "It ain't your fault that we've had so many prisoners crash out of the holding pens."

"Equipment failure was proved, *proved* to be the cause in each and every jailbreak! You can't hang that on me."

"Sure, you're covered."

"You're so smart, Sugarland, suppose you go to Sheriff Thornton and ask him to send us some hardware that really works, for a change."

"Well, no, Mr. Benedict, I don't believe I'll do that."

"You're damned right you won't, and I'll tell you why. Because if you did, Thornton would chew you a new asshole, boy! The county's barely got the juice to keep this post open and pay our salaries. You go down to the commissioners courthouse with a mouthful of gimmes and a handful of complaints and they'll toss you out on your ear. They'd just as soon close down this station as not, and if they do, we'll both be out of a job. I don't know about you, but I'm too old to have to go to work for a living."

"Speaking of Sheriff Thornton, shouldn't we contact HQ, let 'em know what's happening?"

"Let's get the situation under control first," Benedict said.

Inputting new commands into the surveillance system, he ordered one of the topside spy-eye cameras to execute a slow pan from face to face across the mass of caged men. The ever-changing display flowed across the multiscreen monitors.

"Who else is in the bird cage besides Barton?" he asked, sitting hunched forward, squinting at a screen.

"That sad-eyed fellow with the mustache looks a little like Homicide Roldan," Clem said.

"Hell, it is him! He was supposed to have been killed somewhere down in Mexico last year . . ."

The spy-eye moved on to the next man, and the next, unrolling a veritable rogue's gallery across the screens. Outlaws, gangsters, racketeers—killers all. And no small fry. To a man they were all certified public enemies.

"The FBI must've done it," Clem said at last, a bit dazed. "They're the only outfit around with the smarts and firepower to round up this bunch of bad boys."

"It wasn't them. If this was a fedgov show, they wouldn't be wasting their time with the likes of us. They'd be too busy hogging all the glory for themselves. No, it's not federal," Benedict said.

"Maybe it's a trap," he added, after a pause.

"Mighty expensive bait, Mr. Benedict. Who'd go to the trouble of rounding up some of the most dangerous criminals in Texas just to lay a trap for you and me? Heck, it'd be a lot cheaper just to drop a neutron bomb on us."

"That probably comes next."

"Where there's traps there's usually trappers, but danged if I can find any," Clem said.

"That doesn't mean they're not out there, just that you can't find them. Besides which, this horseshit old hardware we're saddled with couldn't find a prairie fire if it was in the middle of it."

"All clear on the proximity range finder. No aircraft, land cars, spy rays, energy flows, nothing," Clem reported. "No people, either, except for the prisoners."

"Sure, the locals are all dug in in their holes, waiting for the deal to go down so they'll know which way to jump. They'd just as soon see us blasted to kingdom come, the bastards."

"Oh, I don't know about that. I've met a few nice folks in town."

"You must've been looking through a microscope to find them. Why, when Jonesy was killed—Jonesy was your predecessor here as assistant deputy—"

"I know who he is. Was," Clem said.

"He was killed a while back, murdered in the line of duty while protecting the public, mind you. Well, the good people of Beamer Junction didn't even chip in to pay for the funeral. He'd have gone to the body shops to be sold for spare parts if I hadn't stepped in and financed the burial myself. Paid for it out of my own pocket, too."

"That was real big of you, Mr. Benedict."

"Damned straight. But do you think that Sheriff High and Mighty Thornton would authorize the department to reimburse my expenses for seeing to it that a brother officer got a decent send-off? In a pig's ear, he would."

"Poor old Jonesy," Clem said. "Got killed in one of them jailbreaks, didn't he?"

"That's right. Want to make something out of it?"

"No, sir. I just don't want to make the same mistake he did, whatever that was."

"He started thinking he was deputy sheriff material."

"Oh."

Shrugging, Clem switched on a wave-pulse generator and triggered a burst. Topside, a funnel-shaped projector fired an energy beam at the cage. The beam was invisible, but the prisoners could feel it, an unseen force that tingled their flesh, rattled their bones, and made their hair stand on end. Some of them started shouting and screaming.

The beamed wave-pulse was harmless to flesh and blood, but would instantly activate the detonator of any bomb in its path, causing it to explode. A useful device for dealing with concealed logic-chip "smart" bombs and mines, booby traps, and other infernal machines.

No bombs were planted among the prisoners, the cage, or its environs. Otherwise the beam sweep would have set them off with a blast.

The prisoners who had panicked settled down and fell silent when they realized they were going to live, for a little while longer, at least.

"Chickenshits," Mars Barton said, sneering at the four of his fellow prisoners who had succumbed to stark fear. It was the first word he had spoken since waking up hours earlier to find himself bruised, battered, and behind bars.

"If there was a bomb aboard we'd have all been blown to atoms long before you could even feel the wave beam," he said. "Dumbasses."

"You don't look so smart yourself, caged up in here like the rest of us," Marco said. He was sharp-faced, jockey-sized.

"I'm going to kill you for that."

"Yeah? How, by remote control?"

"Every man, woman, and child I ever put on my list died. Every one. You're on my list, Marco."

"Big man. Let's see how tough you are when they seal you into that death chamber, big boy."

"No jail can hold the Red Planet Man."

"Big talk."

"I'm going to kill you, Marco."

"All you big guys are yellow down deep, when the crunch comes. It's a known fact," Marco said.

"Shut up, both of you pigs," Homicide Roldan said.

"You're dead," Barton said, not skipping a beat. "I'm going to kill you for calling me a pig, Roldan."

"I kill you first, you pig."

"Save it for the guy who put us in here," somebody said.

That gave them all something to think about. Gloom fell on the group, silence. Mars Barton was the first to break the hush.

"I'll kill him, too, the longest and hardest kill of them all," the Martian said. "Only—who is he?"

"That's what we'd all like to know," Action Man Blugeld said.

"You're the guy with all the answers, Skintop. Any ideas as to who put the arm on us?" Marco said.

Skintop was hairless from head to toe, with a pear-shaped face and a physique to match.

"I'm as much in the dark as the rest of you boys, but I can tell you this," he said. "Whoever he is, this mystery man's no friend of ours."

"No shit, Sherlock. I figured that one out by myself," Marco said.

"Then what'd you ask me for?"

"I know who he is," Niles Visser said.

"Bullshit," Marco said.

Addiction to the dangerous snythetic hormone Ferol had turned the whites of Visser's eyes red and his gums purple. His yellow teeth had been filled into sharp points. As a member of the Chrome Mau Mau secret society, he followed their custom of cutting a notch in his ears for each of his kills. He had had so many kills that both of his ears were fringed on the edge all the way around. It would not be pleasant when his current dose of Ferol began to wear off, but the redness of his eyes indicated that that time was yet to come.

"I know," he said.

"Yeah? How about letting the rest of us in on the secret?"

"He's the Man, Marco."

"What kind of jiveass double-talk is that?!"

"The Man, Sam, that's what he am. The Man with a plan. Law man, gun man, kick-ass man. The Man."

"He sure whomped our butts," somebody said.

"That's why he's the Man," Visser said. "The Big Boss Man."

"Somebody's got to go topside and you're elected, Sugarland."

"I'll be done suiting up in a minute, Mr. Benedict."

"No hurry. Those crooks aren't going anywhere. Let them stew for a while, it's good for them. The heat will cook some of the poison out of them."

Benedict occupied the command chair of the control console. Rows of instrument panels were set back in steps atop the massive mechanism, stacked like the keyboards of an old-fashioned church pipe organ. Two tiers of viewscreens rose from the top of the console.

Benedict fingered the handgrips of his set of controls for the weapons firing system. The safeties were on, Clem noticed, while trying to seem as if he weren't paying attention to such things.

"I'll cover you from here with the big guns," Benedict said. "If it's a trap, I'll open up and turn those crooks into chopped meat!"

Slowed by battle armor, Clem clumped to his customary sideman spot at the console and ponderously lowered himself into the chair.

"This is no time to be sitting down on the job," Benedict said.

"Can't fix these battle boots standing up."

Reaching down, Clem began fiddling with the adjustable straps and buckles of his cumbersome antishock boots.

"Reach headquarters yet?" he asked.

"No, I'm still trying to get through."

"That's funny, they were coming through loud and clear just a few hours ago."

"Signals are always stronger at night. Maybe a local magnetic storm is blocking our transmission. Or maybe it's a glitch somewhere in our equipment. I'll attend to it directly."

"I'd sure feel a whole lot better if HQ was in on this thing, just in case something goes wrong. At least then we'd have our asses covered with the higher-ups."

"Hell, boy, if something goes wrong you won't have any ass left to cover! But don't worry. From where I sit, we've got the situation under control."

"From where you sit—yeah."

"Senior man's always the last to leave his post, Sugarland. That's departmental standard operating procedure."

"It's also SOP to report any unusual activity to headquarters ASAP. And if having ten big-shot crooks drop in on us out of the blue ain't unusual, I don't know what is!"

"ASAP means As Soon As Possible, Sugarland. I can't report until the comm system starts cooperating again."

"Why don't I give it a try? I'm a pretty fair hand with a broadcast beam, if I do say so myself,"

Clem started to rise from his chair, but Benedict motioned for him to sit back down.

"Finish what you're doing. You've got important work to do topside. I'll give headquarters another try."

"Okay, Mr. Benedict."

Benedict swiveled his chair to the left so he was facing the comm system's instrument board. He fiddled with switches and turned dials, producing a variety of electronic wheeps, beeps, and whoops that were counterpointed with the wash of hissing static coming through the speaker grids. He sat in such a way that his body blocked Clem's view of what his hands were really doing on the controls.

But that put his back to Clem, too, so he couldn't see what his assistant was doing. Glancing sideways to make sure that Benedict was fully occupied, Clem reached down as if to readjust the fastenings of his boots. Instead, he ran his fingers along the underside of the console's overhanging kneehole flange until he found a small stud, about the size of a nailhead. He pressed it. A hinged lid swung open and downward, exposing a recessed space that was roughly the size and shape of a brick. The lid unlatched with a click, but Benedict didn't hear it over the surflike noise of the static.

The space was a fusebox, one of a row of them located for easy access under the console overhang. Making sure that Benedict was still occupied with the balky communicator (or pretending to be), Clem reached into the box and removed a few key fuses, tiny clear plastic tubes with hairlike wire filament cores. Palming the fuses, he closed the fusebox lid and straightened up in his seat. Benedict was none the wiser.

"Any luck reaching HQ?" Clem said.

"I'm making progress," Benedict said over his shoulder. He lowered the volume control, muting the static to a low background hiss.

"The interference seems to be dying down. Probably a local mag storm, like I said. I should be able to punch through a beam in a few more minutes," he said. "Ready to go topside, Sugarland?"

"Yes, sir."

"Well, get to it, then. I want to be able to tell HQ that we've got the situation well in hand."

Clem rose, making for the armory at the opposite end of the command post. He crossed the circular floor of the station 's cylindrically shaped central core, his heavy footfalls echoing through the silo-like shaft. Battle armor restricted his movements, causing him to move in a loose-jointed, shambling stance with his heavy-booted feet spread far apart to maintain better balance.

A sidelong glimpse of the comm system board confirmed his suspicions: the settings were all wrong to send a transceiver beam to headquarters. Benedict was just going through the motions, pretending to be trying to send a message.

Two can play at that game, Clem thought, feeling the filched fuses nestled comfortably in the palm of his left hand.

He input the armory access code on a keypad, unlocking the ponderous hatch door. The armory was built like a bank vault—better, in fact, since weapons were more valuable than money in the savage world of A.D. 2035.

Unsealed, the massive door swung outward and open. It was six feet in diameter and three feet thick, made of compound layers of metalloy and super-strength ceramics. Clem had to duck his head as he stepped through the hatchway into the vault. Long guns and hand weapons hung in racks on the walls; floor bins held quantities of cartridges, replacement charge clips, special task rounds, bolt-on laser target-finders, and other lethal options. A separate case stored a variety of crowd-control shells: gas, irritant powder, blister fog, Vomex, sub- and hyper-sonic "screamer" pellets. A few extra battle armor suits hung on hooks on the back wall, and a tripod-mounted light machine gun sat on the floor in the corner. All the station's conwep—conventional weaponry—was here, except for the Q-gun ammunition, which was stored in the big gun's turret.

Clem put the fuses in a safe place in the medikit box clipped to his utility belt. He then armed himself with an assault rifle, equipped with an underslung shock-charge beamer, and a holstered pair of machine pistols, which he belted onto his hips. To his utility belt he secured a bulletproof box, filled with spare ammo clips, and two grenades, one smoke and one flash-concussion. Almost as an afterthought, he added a high explosive (HE) grenade to his armaments.

Slinging the rifle over his shoulder and holding a helmet under one arm, he exited the armory vault and resealed it.

"Nothing new to report, except that our caged birds are getting a whole hell of a lot hotter now that the sun's coming up," Benedict said.

Seeing Clem eyeing the transceiver, he added, "I had HQ for a few seconds but I lost them. That mag storm must be a big one."

"Must be."

Clem ran a commo check on the mini-transceiver built into his helmet. It worked fine. Donning the helmet, he secured the bottom of it to the notches and grooves of the ring collar of his armored torso protector. A slight turn to the left locked it in place with an airtight seal. He kept his visored face-plate raised, not wanting to tap into the suit's canned air until the last possible second.

"Well, here goes nothing," he said.

"Cheer up! Think of how much worse it would be if you had to go up against any one of those fellows if he wasn't caged. Besides, if things work out, you're going to be a rich man. We both will. You can use your share of the reward to buy your own station and then you can be the boss," Benedict said.

Clem picked up his gauntlets and crossed to the elevator. A spiral staircase wound around a central axis pillar to the upper levels, but it was basically an auxiliary fallback option in case an emergency should incapacitate the elevators.

Clem pressed a button, the doors opened, and he entered the car. He pressed another button to go to the top level.

"There's a commendation in this for you for sure, maybe even a medal," Benedict was calling to him as the elevator doors slid shut.

Clem stepped off at the top floor, the car doors automatically *whooshing* shut behind him. He was in a loftlike space, a single room whose ceiling was the curved dome at the top of the station which protruded above ground. No windows broke the uniformity of its smooth walls, to maintain the greatest structural integrity against bombs, bullets, beams, and burners. Viewscreens on a console rising from the floor at the center of the room were video windows on the outside world.

Clem fitted his hands inside the gauntlets, whose tops fastened to the ring cuffs of the fleximesh sleeves of his armor, forming an airtight seal to protect against airborne toxic agents.

He lowered his face-plate, his suit's self-contained oxy supply switching on the instant that the visor was sealed into place. The bottled air was oxygen-enriched but tasted flat with that stale, "canned" flavor given it by the high-compression tanks. It sure beat inhaling a double lungful of deadly nerve gas or viral bio-spray, though.

Pausing to finetune the helmet's audionics, he boosted the pickup on the exterior mikes and lowered the volume of Benedict's transmissions.

He went to the airlock opposite the elevator from which he had emerged. The dogs unlocked; the hatch opened. Clem entered the chamber. The hatch closed and the autodogs battened down, locking it.

The airlock was similar in size and shape to an old-fashioned diving bell. The terror tactics of the times demanded that any paramilitary installation that wanted to stay in business must be protected against contamination from Chemical and Biological Warfare agents. CBW had been used extensively in most of the major and minor global conflicts of the last forty years. A lot of CBW surplus hardware was left over from the last war, and it wasn't that hard to make from scratch, either.

Pumps chugged as the airlock began cycling. Red warning lights shone as the air was sucked out of the chamber. Pneumatic tubes veining Clem's bodysuit like a circulatory system inflated, compensating for the decrease in air pressure. Still, the sensation was uncomfortable. Not for the first time, Clem thought about how the airlock would make a pretty fair death chamber, especially since the controls could be overridden by the station's command console down below.

That was why he had brought along the HE grenade. If for some reason the hatches refused to open, as a last resort he could blast them open with the grenade. Who knows? He might even survive the explosion, thanks to his armor.

But there were no tricks, no surprises. High-pitched whistling sounded as the outside air was gradually bled into the low-pressure chamber. The unpleasant sensation lessened until pressure was restored to normal.

His suit-mounted sensors detected no traces of CBW toxic agents in the outer air, leaving the helmet's internal warning buzzer unsounded and the alarm lights unlit. Good. But he was keeping his suit sealed. He had never had to suit up to this extent to go topside before, except for a few rare occasions when the station was on full battle alert—false alerts.

And this time?

Green go lights flashed on the display board over the top of the hatch, replacing the red lights. Clem threw the release. The hatch unhooked and swung up and outward, opening on a passageway, a slab-sided corridor about ten feet long and eight feet high. The muzzle of Clem's shoulder-slung rifle missed grazing the ceiling by a few inches. Overhead, inset disc-shaped glow panels spaced at regular intervals shed a watery, cheerless light.

The corridor ended in a massive metal portal. Clem activated the unlocking mechanism. Hidden motors, unseen but heard, lowered the foot-thick blast-proof door out and down, like a drawbridge. Meanwhile, Clem had slung down his rifle so that he held it waist-high in both hands, leveling the muzzle.

The drawbridge touched ground, settling itself lengthwise with the dull thudding boom of a couple of tons of metal nestling into terra firma.

Clem stepped outside, into the open.